BOOK NEWS

Sign up for exclusive updates and offers at
news.jljarvis.com

A COWBOY KIND OF LOVE

A COWBOY KIND OF LOVE

J.L. JARVIS

A Cowboy Kind of Love

This book is a work of fiction. Names, characters, places and incidents are products of the author's imagination or are used fictitiously. Any resemblance to actual events, locales, or persons, living or dead, is entirely coincidental.

Printed in the United States of America
First Printing, 2026
ISBN 978-1-942767-93-0

Published by Bookbinder Press
BookbinderPress.com

CHAPTER ONE

THE RAIN HAD BEEN COMING down since Monday.

By Wednesday, Bobby Tapley had begun to take it personally.

She sat at her desk in the second bedroom of her Tarrytown apartment, the one she'd converted into an office when she no longer needed a guest room because the guests had stopped coming. As it turned out, her friends had actually been Ted's friends. Her own were scattered across Manhattan and an hour away by Metro-North, both of which seemed a world away from the quiet streets and bare March trees of a town she'd moved to for a man who had since moved on without her.

The photographs on her screen weren't helping. The Whitfield-Kessler wedding was last Saturday, and now she had 281 images of someone else's best day. Having shot forty-seven weddings in the past eighteen months, she could now distinguish tulle from taffeta at a glance.

Frame 112 stopped her.

Ted was in it. Not centered, not the subject, but just there at the edge of the dance floor in his groomsman's suit with his sleeves rolled to the elbows, laughing at something the best man had said. His head was tipped back, and his teeth were showing, and he looked like a man who was having a very good time at a party where his ex-girlfriend was being paid to stand in a corner and document it.

She'd booked this wedding a year ago. Ted had recommended her to the bride back when he and Bobby were still a thing, and recommending your girlfriend for a friend's wedding was the kind of generous, thoughtful gesture he was good at. By the time the wedding actually arrived, they'd been apart for five months. She couldn't back out without burning a professional bridge she couldn't afford to lose. So she went. She stood behind her camera, documenting someone else's happiness while she did the work. She did it well because she always did it well.

She'd done her best to keep him out of frame where she could, but he was a groomsman. He was in the formal shots, the processional, and the toasts. He was on the dance floor with a woman Bobby didn't recognize, his hand at the small of her back, looking down at her with an expression Bobby remembered receiving and would rather not have been reminded of.

She dragged frame 112 into the keepers folder because it was well-composed and the bride's mother, who was paying for the photographs, was in the background. Professional standards prevailed. Personal feelings didn't count.

She reached for her coffee. Stone-cold. She'd made it two hours ago, which meant she'd been sitting in gray March light for two hours, sorting wedding pictures while the rain tapped at the windows and the apartment taunted her with its silence. The kitchen faucet dripped at intervals she could almost predict. The heat cycled on, ran for eight minutes, and clicked off. In the living room, the books sat in the same order they'd been in since October, when she'd reorganized them by color because she'd needed something to do with her hands on a Sunday that stretched out ahead of her with nothing in it.

She used to travel. That was the bitter part, the part she tried not to look at directly. Before Ted, she'd shot editorial work in Morocco, Newfoundland, and the Outer Banks. Magazines called, and she went. She loved the work and the adventure. Then she met Ted, and she stayed. She turned down a ten-day assignment in Nova Scotia because he'd planned a weekend in the Berkshires. She passed on a feature in Savannah because it conflicted with his company retreat, and he'd wanted her there. The small choices felt like love at the time but looked like something else from this distance. Editors she'd said no to twice didn't call a third time. They found other photographers, ones who answered their phones and got on planes.

Now she shot weddings, corporate events, and the occasional garden party for a lifestyle magazine that paid on time and never required her to leave the tri-state area. The work covered her rent, kept her name in circulation, and did not, under any circumstances, require her to feel anything.

She had a good life. She reminded herself of this on a regular basis, the way a person checks a parking meter. Good apartment, adequate income, and great coffee, when she remembered to drink it hot. The gap between good enough and actually good was something she tried not to examine on rainy Wednesdays.

She scrolled past three more frames of Ted and dragged them into the folder without looking too closely.

Her phone buzzed on the desk.

Kay Briggs: Bobby! Calling you in five.

Kay's texts always arrived like stage directions. Bobby barely had time to push her computer glasses up into her hair before the phone rang.

"Good morning," Bobby said.

"Good morning, and I need you in Texas." Kay had the energy of someone who ran a regional magazine, two Substacks, and three ongoing vendettas with her layout department. For four years she'd been Bobby's most reliable editor and the closest thing to a professional best friend she had left. "My photographer bailed. Appendectomy. The nerve! The point is, I have a feature shooting and no one behind the camera."

"Texas," Bobby said, unsure of how she felt about the idea, having never been there.

"Hill Country. A family called the Cavanaughs. Third-generation cattle ranch, about two thousand acres, spring-fed creek, heritage beef operation. My writer's been out there a week, and he's already calling it the best piece of his career. I need photographs that deserve that piece."

Bobby carried her cold coffee to the window. The Tarrytown winter stared back: gray sky, wet pavement, bare trees, and one determined forsythia trying to bud. Across the street, the neighbor's house sat dark. They were in Florida until April. Half of Tarrytown was somewhere else until April.

"A cattle ranch," she said.

"A working cattle ranch. Cowboys, horses, the whole situation. A big limestone farmhouse and about two hundred fifty head of cattle. Have you seen Yellowstone?"

"No."

"Well, it's like that, but less murder, more mucking stalls." Kay knew Bobby well enough to pause before delivering the close. "The older brother is the main contact. Wyatt Cavanaugh. My writer described him as 'a man of few words, most of them pointed.' Take that as you will."

"I'll manage," Bobby said.

"You always do. Listen, it's two weeks. The wildflowers are blooming. The sun is shining. And the story is real, Bobby. This is a family holding on to something when the whole industry is trying to shake them loose. A whole way of life, slipping away while nobody's paying attention." Kay paused. "This isn't weddings."

That struck a chord. Kay knew about the Whitfield-Kessler wedding and Ted. She knew exactly where to put pressure, which was what made her good at her job and occasionally impossible to refuse. Bobby looked at the forsythia buds and thought about sunshine. She thought about open land and the long shadows of late afternoon across grass, about a sky she'd only seen in paintings of the American West. She thought about two weeks in a place that wasn't this apartment, this town, or this tidy life which, since Ted, she'd been tending like a window box that wouldn't bloom.

"When do you need me?" she said.

"Day after tomorrow. I'll email the itinerary. You'll fly into Austin and drive from there, about two hours into the Hill Country." A pause. "Bobby. Thank you."

After they hung up, the apartment was quiet with anticipation of a decision she hadn't had time to completely consider. Bobby stood at the window and let it settle. She had a job that wasn't a wedding or a corporate mixer in a hotel ballroom. She was going somewhere real, with land and sky, and a story worth shooting.

She went back to her desk. On the screen, there was Ted's face again, still laughing, still having the time of his life. She looked at him for a moment. Then she finished the edit, flagged the keepers, and closed the folder.

She pulled up Kay's email, already waiting with the flight details and a phone number.

> Wyatt Cavanaugh. Cavanaugh Creek Ranch. Text or call to confirm your arrival.

Bobby typed the text before she could overthink it.

> Mr. Cavanaugh, this is Bobby Tapley, Kay Briggs's replacement photographer. I can be there Friday afternoon if that works with your schedule.

The reply came twelve minutes later. She knew because she'd been staring at the screen for eleven of them.

> Friday works. I'll have Judd set up the bunkhouse. You'll be in with the hands. Nothing fancy, but it's clean. Be here by 6 o'clock. Watch for the creek crossing—flooded last week.

Bobby read it twice. *You'll be in with the hands.* Well, it wasn't a five-star hotel, but she'd slept in worse. She hoped.

Bobby set the phone down and looked at it. There were maybe thirty words total, half of them logistical, the other bone-dry. She already knew one thing about Wyatt Cavanaugh: he didn't waste words.

She opened a new note and started her packing list. Camera bodies: the Canon R6 and the backup. Lenses: the 24-70, the 70-200, and the wide prime she kept meaning to use more. Batteries, cards, and the portable hard drive. Laptop, charging cables, and extra USB cords, because she always forgot at least one.

Clothes were a different question. She inventoried her wardrobe and came up short. Jeans and T-shirts would do, but footwear was a problem. She had ankle boots and ballet flats for everyday wear, heels for gallery openings, and running shoes for the river trail, none of which belonged on a cattle ranch. Too late for delivery. She'd figure it out in Austin, along with a hat if she could find one that didn't make her look like Jessie from Toy Story.

She was pulling the carry-on out of the closet when the Morocco print caught her eye. A doorway in Marrakech: a slant of afternoon sun on white plaster, the shadow of a man she'd never gotten a name for. She'd taken it during a week alone, the last trip she'd made before Ted, back when being alone still felt like freedom rather than a chronic condition she was learning to manage.

She pulled the carry-on onto the bed, laid out her lenses in a row, and folded three pairs of jeans, three T-shirts, and a flannel shirt. She'd wear her Chelsea boots, which, while sturdy and waterproof, were completely wrong for Texas. But they were what she had.

She zipped the bag, stood back, and looked at it. One suitcase and two camera bags. That was what her life came down to. Everything she truly needed fit on a full-sized bed with room to spare.

She picked up her phone and texted Kay:

Confirmed with Cavanaugh. I'm off to Texas.

Kay's reply was immediate.

You're going to love it!

Bobby put the phone down. She'd believe that when she saw it.

LINDSEY MORAN WAS ALREADY at a second-floor table when Bobby arrived at their favorite restaurant. Through the window, the Hudson spread out wide and silver. Lindsey. She had a glass of white wine and the look of a woman who'd taken the 11:40 Metro-North from Grand Central specifically so she could give her best friend a proper sendoff.

"You look packed and ready to go," Lindsey said.

"How can you tell?"

"You've got that expression. Like you just finished a to-do list and you don't know what to do with your hands." She pushed the bread basket across the table. "Eat. You won't get sourdough like this in cattle country."

Bobby sat down and tore off a piece. Through the window, the river moved slowly beneath a pale sky. A freight barge glided through the water near the Tappan Zee, and the far shore was still bare-branched and brown, as if March were holding on with both hands.

"So," Lindsey said. "Texas."

"Texas."

"A cattle ranch."

"A working cattle ranch. Two thousand acres, beef, cowboys. The whole thing."

Lindsey's eyes went wide and bright. "Cowboys."

"And livestock. Cows. Fences. Dirt."

"Cowboys, though."

"I'm going to photograph cattle, not date them."

"The cattle aren't what I'm talking about, and you know it." Lindsey pointed a piece of bread at her. "You'd better pack one and bring him back for me."

Bobby picked up the menu. "I'm ordering."

"I'm just saying. If there happens to be a rugged, emotionally unavailable man in a pair of worn-in jeans who looks good on a horse—"

"I'm reading the specials now."

"—you owe it to our friendship to at least take a picture."

The waiter came, and Bobby ordered the salmon and a glass of whatever Lindsey was drinking, and for a few minutes they talked about other things. Lindsey's week at the salon. A bride who'd changed her hair three times the morning of her wedding and then cried through the ceremony anyway. The radiator in Lindsey's apartment, which had started making a sound she described as "an axe murderer practicing for an upcoming job on the pipes."

It was easy, the way it always was with Lindsey. They'd met five years ago at a wedding in Cold Spring, with Lindsey doing hair and makeup for the bridal party, while Bobby was behind the camera. The bride's sister had fainted during the first look, and they'd spent twenty minutes together in a hallway, Lindsey fanning the sister with a program while Bobby went for water, and by the end of the reception, they'd exchanged numbers and made dinner plans that actually happened.

Lindsey had come into Bobby's life when Ted was

already in it, and she'd had the good grace never to say what Bobby suspected she'd always thought, which was that Ted was a decent man who simply wasn't all that interested in being a great one.

Lindsey had seen it the way hairdressers see things, from years of sitting behind a chair while people talked about their lives. She'd developed a quiet radar for the difference between a man who was present and a man who was just in the room. She never said a word about Ted while they were together. The night it ended, she showed up with wine and takeout and didn't say a word about Ted then, either. She just sat on the couch and let Bobby talk until she ran out of things to say.

"The timing's good, though," Lindsey said now, in the way she had of circling back to a subject she'd never actually left.

Bobby knew what she meant. "It's a work assignment."

"Sure."

"It *is*."

"I said sure." Lindsey's mouth twitched. "But also the timing's good. Getting out of here for a couple of weeks. Different scenery. Different air." She looked out at the river and then back at Bobby. "You need this."

Bobby didn't argue because Lindsey wasn't wrong. Since Ted, the apartment had contained the quiet life she'd built to exact specifications, and somewhere along the way, the specifications had become a cage she'd designed herself. Two weeks on a ranch in Texas wasn't going to fix anything. But it was progress. It wasn't the same four walls and the same view of the same street.

"It's going to be great," Lindsey said. "Sun. Open sky. You'll come back with gorgeous pictures and a tan."

"I don't tan. I freckle, and then I peel."

"So you'll come back with gorgeous pictures." Lindsey lifted her glass. "To Texas."

Bobby touched her glass to Lindsey's. "To Texas."

They finished lunch slowly, the way people do when they know it's the last unhurried afternoon they'll have together for a while. Lindsey talked about a destination wedding she had coming up in Savannah, and Bobby told her about the magazine feature Kay had described. The family was holding on to a ranch that had been in their family for generations, while the industry tried to shake them loose. Lindsey listened the way she always listened, with her full attention.

Outside, the river caught a break in the clouds and turned silver-white for a few seconds before going gray again. Bobby watched it and thought about a creek in Texas she'd never seen.

They split the check and walked out into the afternoon. The air was raw and damp with the wind off the river. Lindsey pulled her coat tighter and turned to Bobby on the sidewalk.

"Call me when you get there."

"I will."

"I mean it. I want to hear everything: the ranch, the cattle, the hot cowboy."

"There is no hot cowboy."

"There's always a hot cowboy because cowboys are hot. They can't help it." Lindsey gave her a hug. Then she was walking toward the station, one hand raised without looking back.

Bobby walked home, feeling every bit of the damp chill in the air. But tomorrow she'd be in Texas beneath the warm sun.

She thought about what Lindsey had said. "You need this."

She turned onto her street and looked at her building. On the second floor, third window from the left, was her apartment where she lived her orderly life. In the window box, the winter herbs she'd planted in October were gray, brown, and mostly dead.

She went inside and checked her bags one more time. Then she set her alarm and went to bed early, lay in the dark, and listened to the rain start up again, soft, steady, and familiar. Tomorrow she would leave it behind.

She made it to LaGuardia in good time on Friday morning: long-term parking, twenty minutes through TSA PreCheck, and then the familiar walk to the lounge.

The lounge was half-empty. A man in his fifties stood behind the bar, calmly polishing glasses.

His name tag said Earl. She remembered him from the last three times she'd been here.

Bobby went to the bar.

"What'll it be?" Earl asked.

"Prosecco," she said. Then, because it was eleven in the morning and he was looking at her with the nonjudgmental demeanor of a seasoned bartender. "Where are you off to?"

"Texas."

"First time?"

"Yeah."

He poured the glass and set it in front of her. "Texas is something."

"So I keep hearing."

"My daughter went to UT." He held up a hand with the index and pinky fingers extended.

"Hook 'em horns," he said by way of explanation.

She lifted her glass. "Okay." She had absolutely no idea what it meant, but she felt like she should play along.

She took her Prosecco to the window seat. Outside, the tarmac was still wet from the morning rain and reflected the sky in long silver sheets. Two luggage carts moved between the gates. A regional jet sat at the far end of the concourse, and the light, overcast but thinning, came in flat and caught the wet pavement so that the planes looked like they were floating on silver water.

Bobby reached into her bag. She told herself she was only going to check the settings.

She lifted her Canon R6 toward the window, found the reflection of the sky in the wet tarmac, and took one frame. Then a second one, because an airport employee in an orange vest walked across the reflection, and the geometry was too clean to pass up.

She capped the lens. Two frames were enough.

Her phone buzzed.

Final boarding, Gate C7.

She finished the Prosecco in one practical swallow, shouldered her bag, and headed for the gate. At the jetway, she handed over her boarding pass and stepped through. In four hours she'd go from a gray New York morning to sunny Texas in wildflower season.

She found her seat, buckled in, and looked out the window one last time. The clouds were thinning. Blue showed through in long bright strips, wider than anything the Tarrytown sky had offered in weeks.

She leaned her head back and closed her eyes. For the first time in months, the knot between her shoulders eased enough that she realized it had been there all along.

She was on her way.

CHAPTER TWO

The rental was a white Ford Explorer with enough bells and whistles to make the drive on 290 feel like an event. Or maybe it was just the mood she was in. After four months of Tarrytown gray, the wide-open countryside hit her nervous system like a window thrown open in a room that had been closed too long.

The road led out of the Austin suburbs, and the strip malls gave way to scattered cedar and live oak, low and contorted. Their branches grew horizontally and then turned up at the ends, as though the trees had started to reach for something and changed their minds.

Since Kay's call, she'd done her research. She'd looked at the work of other photographers who'd shot the Hill Country, read the landscape descriptions in the magazine piece Kay forwarded, and watched *Giant, Open Range,* and two episodes of *Yellowstone.*

The country she was driving through resembled none of them. This was gentle, rolling land with patches of wildflowers lining the highway and bluebonnets peppering the grass alongside the road.

Before long, the bluebonnets were everywhere, covering whole hillsides in a brilliant violet-blue. She'd seen photographs, but they couldn't replicate what it was like to drive through them with the late sun hitting from the side and the color running all the way to the tree line. She rolled the window down and let the warm air pour into the car.

Kay had forwarded the ranch directions along with a note:

"The last twelve miles will test your faith in the GPS. Trust it."

That was no lie. She left the highway and followed a county road until the pavement ended and gravel began. The gravel road grew narrow enough that the cedar branches on either side seemed to be reaching in through the windows. She checked the GPS twice.

Then the land opened, and she saw the gate.

It was welded pipe, heavy gauge, set between limestone gateposts. Above it, an arch of steel had been worked into the shape of the Cavanaugh Creek Ranch brand: two interlocking C's with a water drop beneath them, rough, handmade, and clearly built to last another hundred years. She got out and opened the gate. A cattle guard ran beneath the gate, its metal pipes rattling under her tires as she rolled across.

After stopping on the other side and closing the gate, she followed the ranch road lined on both sides with live oaks whose canopies arched and met overhead in a low green ceiling. The late light came through in pieces, shifting. After a quarter-mile, she spied a limestone house that sat solid and square on a hill, with a metal roof gone soft and rust-orange with decades of weather. A barn stood to the left, weathered red, and beyond it the pasture opened south toward a line of cypress, willows, and tall pecans that must have been the creek. Cattle moved in the distance, dark shapes drifting through amber grass.

Bobby sat in the idling Explorer with both hands on the wheel and took it all in. She had photographed brownstones in Brooklyn, fishing boats in Newfoundland, and a thousand Manhattan skylines, but none of it had prepared her for what this particular view was doing to her chest. It wasn't beauty, exactly. Beauty, she knew what to do with. This was something quieter. This place looked like it had been here long before anyone with a camera showed up and would be here long after, with no regard for her opinion on the matter.

She took her foot off the brake and drove toward the house, where she parked beside a dusty flatbed near the barn and cut the engine. The silence was immediate and enormous. No traffic, no Metro-North rumble, no neighbors' dogs. Just the faint sound of wind in the live oaks and, somewhere in the distance, a cow calling out.

Bobby got out, stretched, and looked around. The scent of unfamiliar grasses on a gentle breeze soothed her travel-weary senses. The late sun was still above the hills, throwing long shadows from the barn across the packed dirt of the yard.

No one came out.

She stood by the Explorer for a moment, checked her phone for a response to the text she'd sent from the Austin airport telling Wyatt she was an hour out; then opened the hatch. She was reaching for her camera bag when movement at the barn caught her eye.

The barn sat slightly uphill from where she'd parked, and the wide double doors were open to the afternoon. A man walked out of the shadow of the doorway and into the sun, and Bobby's hand stopped on her bag.

He was tall, as if the landscape had to make room for him. He stood in the yard with the full breadth of the Hill Country sky behind him, and the late sun catching the dust on his hat. For a disorienting second, she felt as though she'd never seen a real man before.

Then he moved, and the impression shifted from image to man. He came down the gentle slope toward her with an unhurried stride, his long legs in faded Wranglers worn pale at the knees and thighs. His brown boots were caked with a season's worth of dirt that had no intention of leaving. His chambray work shirt was rolled to the elbows, the fabric soft and faded from washing. Beneath it were the broad, square shoulders of someone who'd spent his adult life lifting things that needed lifting without giving it much thought. His forearms were brown from the sun, with the kind of lean, dense muscle that came from actual work instead of a gym membership. A hat, sweat-stained and shaped by his hands over time, sat on his head as if it had always been there.

With a halter and lead rope in one hand, he was wiping the other on a rag from his back pocket as he walked. His jaw was set, his mouth a straight line, and his eyes, whose color she couldn't tell yet from this distance, were on her, taking inventory with the flat, unhurried attention of a man who assessed things for a living and appeared to make up his mind about most of them before he got within speaking range.

Bobby stood beside her rented SUV, feeling suddenly self-conscious in her black Chelsea boots, Lululemon leggings, black Merino wool T-shirt, and hair wind-tossed from the car ride. As she watched this cowboy come toward her, she understood three things at once: she had not been remotely prepared for Wyatt Cavanaugh, she was going to have to be professional about it, and that was going to take some effort.

He stopped about six feet from her. It was far enough to feel distant, but close enough to talk and see that his eyes were blue. He looked at her, but didn't say anything, which made her acutely aware of her heartbeat.

"Bobby Tapley," she said, because someone had to go first.

"Wyatt Cavanaugh."

His voice was low and unhurried, like everything else about him. He tucked the rag into his pocket, shifted the halter to his other hand, and shook hers. His handshake was firm and brief, and his hand was calloused and warm. The contact lasted as long as a handshake needed to, and not one second more.

His gaze traveled down past her leggings to her feet. The Chelsea boots. One eyebrow lifted, barely, and came back down. He didn't say a word, which somehow made it worse. His own boots were brown leather, worn to the color of the dirt they stood on.

"Ruby fixed up the bunkhouse for you," he said. "Follow me."

She reached for her suitcase, but he'd already taken it. No offer, no inquiry, just a hand on the handle and the thing was off the ground.

She hoisted a camera bag onto her shoulder and followed him up the worn limestone path, her other bag in his hand as though it weighed nothing. He moved through the yard and around the near side of the barn with that same long, certain stride of a man who not only owned the ground he walked on but the surrounding air.

The path led to a long, low building of the same limestone as everything else on the property. The near end had the organized clutter of a working bunkhouse: hooks loaded with rope and canvas, a bootjack by the door, and a bench worn smooth by years of sitting.

Wyatt opened the door at the far end. The room was small, with a bunk bed against the left wall. The lower bunk was made up with white sheets and a navy blue cotton blanket with square corners tucked flat and tight. A small wooden dresser stood by the door, and the window above it faced east, toward the sound of a creek. On the windowsill, in a glass Mason jar, was an arrangement of wildflowers—pink evening primrose and a small bunch of early bluebonnets, freshly opened, their blue almost startling against the white windowsill.

He said, "The bathroom's at the end of the hall."

Wyatt set her bag on the floor, looked around the room as if checking it against a private standard, and turned to go.

"Mr. Cavanaugh." She wasn't sure why she'd stopped him. He turned, and she found herself with nothing particularly useful to say, so she settled for the obvious. "Thank you."

He held her gaze for a moment with cobalt blue eyes that were dangerously disarming. His expression didn't quite soften, but it seemed to ease slightly to a more reserved tolerance, as if he were unsure of how he felt about the arrangement.

"Don't thank me yet," he said, and then left.

She stood in the room and listened to his boots on the path outside, going back toward the barn, until she couldn't hear them anymore. Then she smiled in disbelief and set her camera bags on the floor.

With a glance around her at a narrow twin bed, an east-facing window, and wildflowers from someone she hadn't met yet, she decided she'd had so much worse. There were forty minutes until supper, which meant forty minutes to go outside and follow the light and her instincts.

The late-afternoon sun against the massive, unspoiled horizon struck her differently than she'd expected. Typically, she would already be composing a shot before she felt anything. Here, she felt it first. The sheer scale of the sky took her breath away. Then she took in the light as it raked across the limestone wall of the barn, throwing every crack and weathered groove into relief and turning the live oaks amber at the tips. She stopped trying to think about it and started shooting.

The barn was her favorite: vertical boards, faded red paint, and a gap in the loft door where a barn swallow went in and came back out twice while she stood there. She circled the building slowly, the way she approached any good subject, looking for the angle that told the truth.

She wandered around the south side of the barn and stopped.

There, in a patch of bare earth, sat a smoker. The drum was black, slick with the glazed residue of decades of smoke and rendered fat. The barrel lay horizontal on iron legs that seemed to have taken root in the dirt. It looked so quintessentially Texan.

She crouched and moved around it slowly, eyeing the welded seam where the firebox met the drum, the late light along the hinges, and the blackened steel against the pale limestone dust.

She was shooting the weld seam from below when she heard a footstep and looked up. A man stood nearby; she would guess at least seventy, with facial lines that marked every decade. White hair peeked out from beneath a beat-up, sun-faded hat, while pale blue eyes peered at her, measuring.

He was smiling at her camera.

"Old Smoky gets everyone that way," he said.

"It's amazing." Bobby straightened. "I'm sorry, I was just—"

"Go right ahead." He waved a hand and held it out in the same motion. "Judd Cavanaugh. Wyatt's uncle."

"Bobby Tapley." She shook it.

He looked at the smoker with craftsman's pride. "My daddy and I built her. I was about fifteen. He got the drum from a cousin working the oil patch down south. This was the early seventies, and fifty-five-gallon drums were everywhere in that world. We burned her out first, ran a hot fire through her to clean out whatever the oil company had left in there. Then Daddy cut the lid and welded the firebox on." He paused. "I held things in place while he struck the arc."

She looked at the firebox, the way it sat lower and heavier than the drum, the weld between them thick and permanent. "He was a welder?"

"Oilfield. Spent twenty years on a rig before he came back to the ranch." Judd's voice had the even quality of someone who enjoyed telling a story he'd gladly repeat to anyone willing to listen. "When his hands got too unsteady, I took over. Eventually I got the whole rig." Another pause. "And the brisket recipe."

"Brisket recipe?"

"Judd's Dry Rub." He said it with zero modesty and twinkling eyes. "That's why I'm still here. Without that, they might've kicked me out long ago."

She laughed.

Judd's eyes lost their twinkle as he looked at her boots with the same unhurried inventory Wyatt had done, except where Wyatt had withheld his opinion,

Judd didn't seem to mind sharing. "You're going to need different boots."

"I'm aware," she said.

He laughed and walked toward the house with a quick wave. "Six o'clock," he called back. "Don't be late. Ruby made skillet chicken and corn bread."

Cavanaugh Creek was a quarter mile south of the barn, running east to west through a grove of bald cypress, live willows, and pecan trees whose broad canopies met overhead and dappled the ground with shade. Pecan shells crunched under her boots on the path down to the water. She found the creek by walking toward the low, continuous sound of running water that she'd been hearing everywhere on the ranch without realizing it.

The creek was maybe ten feet across, clear over a pale limestone bed, moving unhurriedly over the rocks.

A great blue heron stood motionless on the far bank in three inches of water. She hadn't seen it at first, because it was the same gray-blue as the afternoon shadow. But when she did, her whole body went still. Slowly, she raised her camera.

The light was going. She had three minutes, maybe four. She thought about the wedding photographs she'd just finished editing two days before. Frame 112, of Ted laughing on the dance floor, was lodged in her brain. Ted could go hang. None of those photos had felt close to this. And the bird had better legs.

The heron moved one foot, placed it with great deliberateness, and went still again. She pressed the shutter. The light shifted. She moved two steps to the right to reframe.

The heron lifted, vast and unhurried, and crossed the creek on slow wingbeats and was gone into the cypress on the other side.

Bobby lowered the camera. The light had turned peach at the horizon and was fading upward into blue. Behind her, the limestone house's windows were lit in a warm yellow.

Six o'clock, Judd had said.

CHAPTER THREE

SHE KNEW before she looked at her phone. The light told her, the way it had gone from amber to rose to the flat, colorless gray that came while she'd been standing at the creek with her eye at the viewfinder, somewhere between the heron and the stars that were beginning to assert themselves over the hills to the east.

She looked at her phone. 6:14.

She went up the bank fast, ducking under the cypress branches, and half-jogged across the pasture toward the house.

The kitchen door was the closest. She pulled it open and stepped inside with her camera still hanging crosswise over her chest.

Four people at the table turned to look at her.

Wyatt, at the head. Judd to his left. A woman she hadn't met yet, who must have been Ruby, sat across from Judd. A teenage boy at the near end looked up with a teenager's lack of urgency.

The skillet was already in the center of the table. The cornbread was cut.

"I'm so sorry," Bobby said. "I was at the creek and I lost track—"

"Have a seat," said the woman, already on her feet and pulling out the empty chair across from the boy. She had Wyatt's dark eyes and a warmth Wyatt apparently hadn't inherited. "I'm Ruby. I kept a plate warm for you." She was already at the stove, lifting the foil off a plate. "I figured you had some unpacking to do."

Not wanting to dwell on her lateness, Bobby said, "I'm sorry, I should have set an alarm." Bobby set her camera bag under her chair and shrugged off her jacket.

"No worries," Ruby said, setting the plate in front of her. Skillet chicken, baked beans, a wedge of cornbread still steaming. "Work happens."

"Around here, work happens a lot," Judd said, without looking up from his plate.

Bobby looked at Wyatt.

He was eating. He hadn't said a word. His complete attention was on his supper, to the point that she wondered if that wasn't a message all on its own. He had no time or patience for Bobby.

She picked up her fork.

The chicken was good. Really good, with a home-cooked, cast-iron goodness she'd never found in New York.

"This is wonderful," she said.

Ruby smiled. It was, Bobby noticed, the same shape as Wyatt's mouth, except Ruby's smiled, while Wyatt's did not. "Mama's recipe," she said. "Mostly. I changed the spice a little. She never used smoked paprika, but I think she'd have forgiven me by now."

"I'm not convinced of that," Judd said.

"Judd," Ruby said.

"Not that this isn't good, but she was particular."

"She was." Ruby reached for the cornbread basket and held it toward Bobby. "Take two. You can't stop at one. I mean, you're allowed, but no one has yet."

Bobby took two.

The boy at the end of the table was apparently named Denny. He was Ruby's son, Bobby gathered, from the way Ruby said, "Denny, don't put that on the table," without looking in his direction as he set his phone face-up beside his glass. He was fifteen or sixteen, lean and long like Wyatt, with his mother's easier expression. He glanced at Bobby's camera bag under the chair with the first sign of actual interest she'd seen from him.

"Is that a Canon?" he said.

"R6."

He considered this. "Do you have a telephoto?"

"The 70–200 is in the bag. The longer glass is in the car."

He nodded in the way of someone cataloging information they planned to return to.

"Denny's been shooting since he was nine," Ruby said. "Cell phone first, then Judd gave him an old DSLR—"

"The kind with film," Judd clarified, "the way God meant it to be."

"You had to give him a film camera."

"It's like vinyl records. The scratches give it character. Same with film."

Ruby smiled as though she'd heard it before. "So now we can't keep him in film."

Bobby looked at Denny. "What do you shoot?"

"Wildlife mostly." He shrugged in a casual way, but the light in his eyes told another story. It mattered to him. "And some landscape."

"The creek?"

"Yeah."

"I was just down there," Bobby said. "There was a great blue heron on the south bank, about thirty feet past where the root system juts out."

Denny's eyes brightened. He looked at the window, as if calculating whether to go see for himself.

Judd said, "It'll be back in the morning. They usually work the same stretch."

Denny looked at him and nodded.

Wyatt refilled his water glass without comment, but Bobby had the impression he'd taken in the exchange. She couldn't have said exactly why she thought so. The man never reacted. He hadn't even looked up.

Judd, she noticed, was watching her in the comfortable, unconcealed way of someone past the age of pretending not to. When she caught his eye, he raised his chin slightly, in the direction of the skillet. She shook her head. Now on her second piece of cornbread, she knew her limits.

After supper, she helped Ruby clear the plates, overriding the protest that she didn't need to. Wyatt had already pushed back his chair and gone out through the screen door, the sound of his boots on the porch and then off it, heading toward the barn for whatever the last hour of ranch work looked like.

"Don't mind him," Ruby said, stacking the dishes at the sink.

"I don't," Bobby said, and tried to mean it.

Ruby looked at her sideways. "He's not unfriendly. He's—"

"Not a talker," Bobby said.

Ruby let out a quick and bright laugh.

Ruby loaded the dishwasher while Bobby gathered the rest of the dishes, then she helped dry the cookware while Ruby washed. Denny vanished in the direction of the living room. Judd reappeared long enough to refill his coffee mug, pronounce the cornbread better than yesterday, and disappear back outside.

By the time Bobby crossed the yard to the bunkhouse, the sky was fully dark, and she had to use her phone's flashlight to light the way.

She stood for a moment in the middle of the path and tipped her head back at the stars.

She thought she had seen stars before, but in the city, there were usually a few bright ones with the moon doing most of the work. What she saw now wasn't that. Above her, the dark sky seemed to stretch out forever, velvety black with pinpricks of brilliant light. She stood gazing at it.

Inside the bunkhouse, she changed into sweats, brushed her teeth, and lay down on the bunk. She left the curtain open on the east window so, through the glass, she could still see the stars.

The cattle had settled for the night to the sound of the cicadas and the occasional moo. Wind moved through the cedar planks of the barn with a dry, papery sound. In the distance, an owl called twice and didn't call again.

She lasted about twenty minutes before she picked up the camera. Just a few shots through the glass, she told herself.

She found the composition: the window frame, the rectangle of sky, and the slope of the hill where it met the stars.

Click.

She adjusted. Tried a longer exposure with the stars trailing slightly, just enough to show they were moving, or she was.

Click.

She couldn't remember the last time she'd longed to photograph the sky. In this place, everything was so vast and simple that she wanted to capture how small and humbling it felt to be here.

She sat on the edge of the bed and looked at the review screen. The window formed a dark frame for the sky beyond, which was magical.

She put the camera on the windowsill where she could reach it. And then, somewhere between the creek and the owl, and the endless darkness outside, she fell asleep.

CHAPTER FOUR

HE WAS up at four thirty, the same as always.

The ranch had its own clock, and after thirty-seven years, Wyatt was in sync without having to think about it. The days started earlier in calving season and later in winter. He pulled on his Wranglers in the dark and went through the kitchen without turning on a light. The coffee he'd set the timer for the night before was ready. He poured a cup and took it onto the porch.

The black sky was fading in the east, where a strip of dark blue was beginning to separate itself from the hills. The cedar was still. The cattle were quiet. He could hear the creek.

He stood there for a few minutes and let the ranch come back to him like a conversation resuming.

A section of the fence in the south pasture needed two new posts. The water tank by the lower gate had been running low since Monday, and he needed to look at the float valve. Diego Gonzalez was coming over from the neighboring ranch today to help move the north herd, which meant Wyatt could get to the east side by Thursday. He ran through it the way he always ran through it, focusing on the numbers the way his father had taught him. You kept the list in your head so nothing got dropped. You didn't panic about the list. You just worked it.

He'd been working the list for seventeen years, since the morning after his father's funeral, when he walked out onto this same porch and understood that the list was now entirely his.

Some items on the list were getting harder to work on.

He went back inside for a second cup of coffee and looked at the folder on the kitchen table. He'd put it there himself three weeks ago, when he finally sat down with the numbers he'd been avoiding. The ranch ran on 247 head, down from over four hundred before the drought forced him to sell. He could have rebuilt the herd by now if the prices had held, but they hadn't. The Argentine import quota had quadrupled in February, Brazilian beef was flooding the market, and the four corporations that controlled the packing industry were paying ranchers less than thirty-seven cents of every dollar consumers spent on beef at the grocery store. He was looking at a margin that didn't cover the note on the south herd. Not this year. Possibly not next.

He didn't open the folder. He knew what was in it.

Ruby had come to him in January with an idea. She had been doing research, the way Ruby did everything: quietly and thoroughly. A national magazine with a large circulation was doing a feature on Hill Country ranches, heritage operations—the kind of places that had been in the same family for generations. She found the contact, looked at the magazine's past work, and put together a case that was, to be honest, better organized than most of his own business plans.

The way Ruby explained it, the magazine piece wasn't just good publicity. It was the first step toward the plan she'd been building for two years: direct-to-consumer beef, a mail-order operation, and a name people would recognize and trust. The kind of brand story that would let them sell their beef for what it was actually worth instead of taking whatever the packers offered.

He said no. He didn't want a stranger on the property with a camera. Someone who would poke around, ask questions, and turn the ranch into a story for people who bought their beef in plastic wrap and had never been within one hundred miles of a feedlot.

Ruby waited two weeks and came back with numbers. The numbers were Ruby's best argument, and she knew it.

He said yes reluctantly and with conditions. Two weeks. Access to the ranch. Then they would leave.

The photographer got sick, and now a replacement was here. Two more weeks. He did it for Ruby, but he wasn't happy about having some city boy named Bobby following him everywhere with a camera. He could already see it: some guy with gelled hair and manicured nails who would ask Wyatt to stand by the fence and look contemplative.

Then the photographer showed up, and the city boy who stepped out of the driver's side of the car was a woman. She stood about five feet six inches, with dark hair that the wind had gotten to, and she stood there looking at the ranch with an expression he hadn't expected. It wasn't the instant appraisal of someone cataloging its rustic remoteness. Bobby, who, with a name like that, couldn't have blamed him for expecting a man, stood completely still, clutching her shoulder bag with one hand and looking completely off-guard.

Then she turned as he came out of the barn, and her expression changed. She collected herself, stuck out her hand, and introduced herself in a voice that was direct and unselfconscious—a woman comfortable in her own skin, soft skin, as it happened.

Bobby Tapley. In city clothes and shoes that were wrong for every surface on the property, except maybe the house.

Bobby was still out with her camera when he pulled Ruby aside while she cooked dinner. "You didn't tell me Bobby was a woman."

Ruby paused long enough to confirm that she knew what she was doing. "I didn't think it mattered."

"Ruby."

"What? She's here to snap pictures, not hoist bales of hay onto a wagon."

He didn't bother to answer, mainly because the honest answer was more complicated than he wanted it to be, and the easy answer would have been a lie. It didn't matter, at least not in the way Ruby meant. He didn't care whether the photographer was a man or a woman. But he'd expected a man. He'd prepared in his mind how the week was going to go. What showed up had undone that entirely, and now he was annoyed about it in a way that even he had to admit was out of proportion.

"Wyatt, Kay vouched for her, and Kay knows what she's doing. Those magazine layouts are gorgeous. So calm down. She'll be good."

"I don't know that. She's been here for an hour."

"And what's she doing? She's off taking pictures. I saw her just now headed down to the creek."

Wyatt clenched his jaw.

"Give her a chance," Ruby said. "That's all I'm asking."

Wyatt walked out to the barn and remained in a foul mood for the rest of the evening, which he blamed on the float valve, the weather forecast, and the general state of the U.S. cattle market.

THAT WAS YESTERDAY. This morning, on the porch with his second cup of coffee, he was still working out how he felt about things.

By 5:45 a.m., he had the float valve diagnosed—a stuck pin, nothing serious—and was walking back across the yard when he noticed the bunkhouse light was on. The east window, lit against the last of the darkness.

He was always the first person moving on the property, except today. He stopped, looked at the lit window, and then went to the barn. He caught Judd coming out on his way to the house for his usual coffee.

"Bunkhouse light's on," Wyatt said.

Judd didn't look up. "She was up before I was."

"Oh." Wyatt envisioned some sort of Princess and the Pea situation with her bunk.

Judd said, "Yup. Out by the fence at first light, snapping pictures."

Wyatt looked toward the fence. There she was. He didn't realize he was staring until Judd said, "She's not hard on the eyes."

Wyatt snapped his head toward Judd, saw the glint in his eyes, and said, "I've got work to do." With that, he turned and strode away.

Judd, who normally took three weeks to decide whether he approved of a new fence post, had apparently decided to approve of this Bobby woman on day one.

Wyatt wasn't so easily swayed. For one thing, she wasn't his type, not that he had a type. He just knew that it wasn't a woman from New York City who'd probably never been within arm's reach of a live cow in her life. She belonged to a world that ran on assignments and deadlines, and people who moved quickly through places without looking at them. She'd be here for two weeks. She'd take her pictures, get her story, and go back to whatever life she'd come from, because that was the arrangement. Whether she was his type had no bearing on anything.

Ruby found him at the barn just after eight.

She had her coffee and the knowing expression she'd been making at him since she was eleven years old. He'd been on the receiving end of that look for twenty-three years.

"She's good," Ruby said.

"You said that last night."

"Judd thinks so, too." Ruby leaned against the stall door. "And Judd doesn't typically warm up to people. You've said that yourself."

He had said that, but he wasn't about to confirm it.

"You were rude last night," Ruby said. "At dinner."

"What? I didn't say anything rude."

There was that look again. "You didn't say anything, period."

He leveled a barely patient look. "It would have been rude to talk with my mouth full."

"Wyatt." Ruby could cram more meaning into one word than anyone else. "Judd said she was down at the creek taking pictures, which is the whole reason she's here. And you sat there and said about fourteen words in an hour."

"I don't have anything to say to a photographer from New York City."

Ruby didn't say a word. She didn't have to. He knew she wasn't just talking about Bobby Tapley's presence as a dinner companion. She was talking about the folder on the kitchen table. At the same time, Wyatt was thinking about the note on the south herd and the back parcel he'd been thinking about for four months. It had been in the family since his grandfather extended the east boundary in 1962. Wyatt couldn't bring himself to sell it. Not yet.

"If she leaves," Ruby said, "we don't get the magazine article. If we don't get the magazine article, we don't get the story to build our brand on. And if we don't get the brand story—"

"I know."

"Then act like it." She pushed off the stall door. "Just be a human being, Wyatt. That's all I'm asking."

She went back to the house.

He stood in the barn and stared at nothing in particular for a while. Judd paused outside the door but said nothing, which was its own kind of commentary.

He rode out at nine on Shadow, the black quarter horse he'd been working for two years. The climb followed the familiar route to the ridge along the east property line. Limestone broke through the grass in pale shelves, and the cedar gave way to open sky as he reached the top.

He stopped and looked out at the ranch.

From up here, it was constant in its presence but never the same. The entirety of it spread out below: the limestone house, the barn, the bunkhouse, the creek line marked by the cypress and the willows, and the south pasture where the herd was grazing this morning. The back parcel lay to the southeast, the big meadow that was carpeted in bluebonnets right now.

He caught sight of her.

A small figure at the far end of the property, she moved along the creek with her camera. Even from this distance, he could tell she was in no hurry. She stopped, crouched, moved a few steps, and stopped again, low to the ground for what must have been five minutes before she stood and walked on without looking back at what she'd been shooting.

It reminded him of the way he moved through the ranch, reading the ground and the grass, taking note of what the land was telling him without having to translate it into words. She was doing the same thing with a camera. He recognized it and wished he hadn't.

He looked at the back parcel.

At two o'clock, he had a call scheduled with the Ag lender. He knew roughly what the lender was going to say because he already knew the numbers. The numbers said to sell the parcel. A hundred twenty acres along a seasonal creek with good grass—the kind of land that would sell fast at a price that would clear the note and give him two years of breathing room.

His grandfather had bought that land in 1962 for one hundred dollars an acre. His father had run cattle on it for thirty years. The creek ran through the middle of it, the same creek he could hear from the porch every morning, the same creek Bobby Tapley was crouched beside right now with her camera aimed at the water. Today, that same land could bring well over seven thousand dollars an acre.

He sat on the horse and looked at it until the sun cleared the ridge behind him and the shadows shortened across the grass.

Down by the creek, she stood up and turned in his

direction with one hand shading her eyes. He had the sudden, irrational feeling that she could see him up here on the ridge. She couldn't. He was too far, and the light was behind him. But she stood there with her hand raised against the sun, and she looked toward the hills before she turned back to the water.

He turned Shadow and headed back down the ridge.

The call was at two. That gave him five hours to find a reason not to do what the numbers said he should.

Somewhere between the ridge and the barn, he thought about the way she'd looked at the ranch when she first stepped out of that white SUV. She'd gone still. Over the years, he'd seen plenty of people set eyes on the ranch for the first time, and most of them talked, but she didn't say a word. She just stood there and took it all in with a look on her face that was stuck in his mind.

It didn't matter. She was here to do a job. He was here to keep the ranch alive. Those two things overlapped for two weeks, and then they wouldn't, and that would be the end of it.

He unsaddled Shadow and put him in his stall with a measure of grain. The horse bumped his shoulder with his head, and Wyatt stood there for a minute with one hand on the warm neck, not thinking about Bobby or anything else.

He had work to do.

CHAPTER FIVE

By day three, she had the rhythm down. She knew where to stand at six in the morning when the light came over the east hills and caught the limestone of the barn in a way that made it glow. She knew the cattle moved south after the early feed and clustered along the creek by midmorning. She knew that Judd's coffee was ready by five fifteen, that Ruby's kitchen smelled like butter and flour by seven, and that Wyatt was already a shadow in the barn by the time anyone else's boots hit the porch.

Most importantly, she knew to stay out of his way. That part she'd figured out on day one.

The mud happened on Sunday.

When Ruby asked Bobby to help carry cases of canning jars from the storage shed behind the smoke-house, Bobby said yes because Bobby always said yes to Ruby. The woman had fed her three meals a day without complaint and never once made her feel like an outsider. It was an easy thing to do for someone who'd been doing things for her since she'd arrived.

The path between the storage shed, and the kitchen ran along the back of the barn, where a waterline had been leaking since the weekend. Wyatt had mentioned it at breakfast in his usual shorthand: "Pipe's seeping behind the barn. I'll get to it Wednesday." Bobby had filed it away and forgotten it entirely. The ground looked solid. It was not. Her left foot went in up to her ankle, and her right foot followed when she tried to pull the first one free. Then she was standing ankle-deep in Hill Country clay the color of rust, holding a case of Mason jars above her head.

Ruby, who was ten feet ahead with the second case, turned around and stopped.

"Oh, honey," she said.

Bobby looked down at herself. Her ankle boots, which had already endured two days of dust, gravel, and whatever was in the corral, were now buried in six inches of red mud that had the consistency of wet cement and no interest in letting go.

Ruby started to laugh. She couldn't help it. The whole picture was too absurd.

"Don't move," Ruby said. "I'll get a board."

"I'm not going anywhere," Bobby said, which made Ruby laugh more.

Ruby set her case down on a dry patch and came back with a plank from the woodpile. She laid it across the mud, and Bobby stepped onto it, one foot at a time, with the sucking sound of the earth reluctantly releasing her boots. She set the jars on the ground and looked at her feet. The boots were caked to the tops with red mud that was already drying in the sun.

"Those are done for the day," Ruby said.

"I think you mean for good."

Ruby looked at her for a moment. "What size are you?"

"Eight."

"I'm a nine. Close enough. Hold on."

Bobby rinsed her boots under the spigot outside while Ruby disappeared and came back with a pair of worn brown ropers, low-heeled and round-toed with the leather softened by wear. They were scuffed at the toe and the left one had a crease across the instep where someone's foot had bent it a few too many times.

"These are my old everyday boots," Ruby said. "They're a little big on you, but they'll hold."

Bobby stepped into them. A full size too large, the heel lifted slightly when she walked, but they were dry.

"How do I look?" she asked.

Ruby tilted her head. "Like you're getting there."

Bobby wore the ropers for the rest of the day. She clomped across the yard to the bunkhouse to change her mud-caked leggings, clomped back out to the pasture with her camera, and spent the afternoon shooting the south fence line with an extra half-inch of boot flopping at the heel with every step. By evening the boots had warmed to her feet, or her feet had given up and adjusted. Either way, she forgot about them, which was probably the point of good boots.

SUNDAY EVENING, after supper, she stepped outside and found Judd on the bunkhouse porch. He was in the wooden chair at the far end with his boots crossed on the railing and a bottle of Shiner Bock in his hand. With a glance her way, he reached into a cooler, pulled out another, opened it on a bottle opener mounted on the porch railing, and held it out toward her.

Bobby sat down in the other chair and took a drink. It was refreshing and good, just like Texas was beginning to feel for her.

They sat in silence for a while. The cattle were settling for the night and the cicadas were tuning up in the grass. From inside the house, she could hear the faint sound of Ruby's radio through the kitchen window playing a country song she didn't recognize.

"How long have you been here?" Bobby asked.

"On this porch?"

"On this ranch."

Judd took a slow pull from his bottle. "Thirty-two years. Came on when my brother was running it. Wyatt's daddy."

She waited, the way she'd learned to wait with Judd. He talked at his own pace, and you didn't rush it.

"Jack was the older one," Judd said. "He had a kind of sense for the ranch. My sense was for cooking, which isn't quite as useful when you're trying to keep two thousand acres in the black." He looked at the hills. "One Tuesday in March, he had a heart attack at the kitchen table. No warning. The next minute, he was gone. Wyatt was up at UT. Two years in. He came home that night and never went back."

"How old was Wyatt?"

"Twenty." Judd let that sit. "Cole was nineteen, already talking about the rodeo circuit. Ruby was in high school. Heath was just a kid." He set the bottle on his knee. "Wyatt didn't ask for it. He just picked it up."

She thought about Wyatt at the barn at five in the morning, the way he moved through the list of things that needed doing without complaint or comment, the way he carried the weight of the place in his posture without seeming to notice it was there. At twenty, he was two years into a degree, but the ranch needed him more than the university did.

Judd was quiet for a moment. He looked south, toward the dark line of trees along the creek. "Jack planted those pecan trees down there the year Ruby was born. Said by the time the kids were grown, the trees would be too, and they'd never have to buy pecans for pie." He took a pull from his beer. "He was right about that, at least."

"Where are they now?" she asked. "Cole and Heath?"

"Cole's in town. Kerrville." Judd paused, and the pause had a particular quality to it, the kind that came before a story someone was deciding whether to tell. "He rode bulls. Professional circuit, six years. Good at it too. Won buckles. Then he got thrown wrong and that was that." Judd tipped his bottle. "He came back. Helps when he can. It's complicated."

"And Heath?"

"Texas A&M. College Station. Studying to be a large-animal vet." The faintest softening crossed Judd's face. "Only Cavanaugh who got to finish. Smart kid. Quiet, like Wyatt, but different."

Bobby took a sip of her beer and looked out at the dark pasture. Three brothers, one ranch, and the eldest holding it together since he was barely more than a kid himself. She understood something about Wyatt she hadn't before. It wasn't just that the ranch was his responsibility, but it had been his responsibility from a young age. He'd shouldered it so long that the weight had become indistinguishable from who he was.

Sensing the conversation had become too weighty, Bobby looked for an exit. "You mentioned a brisket rub when we first met. Seven spices. You said that's why they keep you around."

He looked at her with the same glint in those blue eyes that she'd noticed the first day, equal parts amusement and appraisal.

"Seven spices," he confirmed.

"Are you going to tell me what they are?"

The glint sharpened. "No, ma'am."

She laughed. Judd finished his beer, set the empty on the porch floor, and stood up with the careful economy of a man whose knees had a sense for the weather.

"Night," he said, and went inside.

Bobby sat on the porch with the rest of her Shiner, gazing at the wide, dark sky, and she thought about a twenty-year-old on the morning after his father's funeral, looking out at everything that was now his to hold together.

Monday morning, Wyatt was finishing his breakfast when he said it. "I'm heading into Kerrville after I check the south line. Ruby, you need anything?"

Ruby was at the stove with her back to the table. She didn't turn around. "I'll make you a list." Then, the way a person mentions something they've only just thought of, she added, "Bobby, didn't you say you needed memory cards?"

Bobby looked up from her eggs. She'd mentioned it yesterday, in passing, while Ruby was showing her where the extra towels were kept. She hadn't thought Ruby was listening.

"I do, but I can take my rental. It's no trouble."

"No sense taking two cars into the same town," Ruby said. She said it to the skillet. "You'd be wasting gas. Wyatt can take you."

Wyatt's coffee cup paused halfway to his mouth. He looked at Ruby, who seemed too focused on draining bacon grease out of the skillet to look at Wyatt.

Bobby said, "It's really not—"

Ruby turned around and looked at her with a warm and entirely immovable smile. "Wyatt doesn't mind. Do you, Wyatt?"

The kitchen was quiet. Judd, at the far end of the table, studied his biscuit with the concentration of a man determined to stay out of this conversation.

"I'll be leaving around one," Wyatt said. He picked up his coffee, pushed back from the table, and was through the screen door before anyone could say another word.

Ruby watched him go. Then she turned back to the stove and looked especially busy.

THEY TOOK WYATT'S TRUCK. Bobby climbed into the passenger side and set her bag on the floor between her boots and buckled in. Wyatt started the engine, pulled out of the yard, and turned onto the county road without a word.

The first five minutes were silent. Bobby watched the landscape slide past, sloping hills with wildflowers and green grass running parallel to the highway as far as she could see. The radio was off, the windows were up, and the cab smelled of oil and dirt, like a truck that worked for a living.

She tried once. "How far is it?"

"About forty minutes."

She tried again a few miles later. "Is there a good place to get camera supplies, or should I just look for a Walmart?"

"There's a camera shop on Water Street. A guy named Hank'll have what you need."

Two sentences. Must be a personal best for the guy. She took the win and stopped pushing.

About twenty minutes into the ride, Wyatt reached for the radio and turned it on low. A country music station was playing an old-sounding song she didn't know, with a steel guitar and a voice that sounded like it had lived a hard life. He didn't sing along, tap the steering wheel, or do any of the things people sometimes do if they feel comfortable enough. He just drove, and the music filled the air where conversation didn't, and made the space feel more settled.

They passed a ranch gate with a hand-painted sign that read "LOST CREEK ANGUS." Wyatt gave it a brief and appraising glance.

"You know them?" Bobby asked.

"I went to school with their youngest."

She waited. Nothing else came. She turned back to the window and watched a red-tailed hawk glide above a cut hay field, circling in wide arcs. She wished she had her long lens.

In Kerrville, Wyatt pulled into a parking space on the main street and cut the engine. "I'll be at the feed store and the co-op. Be back in an hour, maybe less." He looked at her for the first time since they'd left the ranch. "You need more time than that?"

"An hour's fine."

He nodded once and got out. Bobby watched him cross the street with an unhurried stride and his hat low against the afternoon sun. He didn't look back.

She found Hank's camera shop on Water Street, exactly where Wyatt said it would be. The owner was a man in his sixties with wire-rimmed glasses and opinions that he didn't mind sharing while she browsed. She bought memory cards and a pack of silica gel packets because the Hill Country humidity had been fogging her viewfinder in the mornings. Hank asked what she was shooting, and she told him.

"The Cavanaugh place." He gave a knowing nod

as though there were more to say, but this time, he refrained.

She walked Water Street for a while after that, past a few pickups angle-parked along the curb. The town was quiet, and storefront awnings were down in the afternoon heat. She passed a bookstore, an antique shop, and a real estate office with ranch listings posted. In the window of the boot shop, a pair of ropers caught her eye, honey-brown with a low heel. She thought about Ruby's boots clomping on her feet, and she went in and bought them.

She was back at the truck ten minutes early and sat in the passenger seat with the door open and her feet on the running board as she scrolled through photos on her camera. She'd shot the south pasture that morning before breakfast, and there was one frame that stopped her. At the creek in early light, the water was so dark and still where it pooled behind a limestone ledge. The far bank caught the first sun through the cypress. The light had that quality she kept trying to describe to Lindsey but failed. It was warm and soft, as if the land had its own way of holding onto the morning and slowly letting it go.

She was still looking at it when Wyatt tossed a bag of feed supplements into the truck bed and opened the driver's side door. He tossed a quick glance at her camera.

"Got what you needed?" he said.

"I did, thanks."

He started the truck and drove back the way they'd come. The same radio station played the same kind of music while the landscape scrolled past the windows.

Neither of them said a word, but the silence felt different. She supposed she'd grown accustomed to it, not that she enjoyed it, but that was just how it was.

THEY GOT BACK in time for supper. Bobby left her camera bag on the porch by the door and went in to wash up. The kitchen was already full of the smell of whatever Ruby had been working on all afternoon, something with cumin, roasted peppers, and the sweet char of cornbread in a cast-iron skillet.

Supper was pot roast with root vegetables from Ruby's garden, cornbread, and a salad that Judd had assembled. The table was full with Ruby, Judd, Wyatt, Denny, and Bobby. The conversation moved the way it always did at this table, in currents that Bobby was learning to read. Ruby kept it going, Judd dropped in a word here and there, and Wyatt listened.

Denny was next to Bobby, which had become his default spot since the first night. He'd been out with his camera that afternoon, and Bobby asked him if he'd found the heron.

"It was there," he said. "Same bank, like Judd said. But it took off before I could get the exposure right."

"What were you shooting at?"

"One-sixtieth. I know it's too slow."

"For a heron, yeah. Try one-five-hundredth minimum. They look still, but their heads move fast. I got some good ones today. Out by the south pasture, down along the creek."

"The morning light?"

"Just after six. Denny, the way it comes through the cypress canopy down there, it's just—" She stopped herself, aware that she was leaning forward, that her hands were moving the way they did when she talked about something she loved. "Sorry. I get carried away."

"No, go ahead," Denny said. He had that look that she'd noticed the first night, with the shrug that didn't match the light in his eyes.

"There's a spot where the creek pools behind a limestone ledge," she said. "And the light was coming in through the trees in these broken shafts. The water was so still that the reflection was almost sharper than what's above it. The far bank was catching the first sun and it turned this color I don't even have a word for. Between gold and amber, it was like the land held onto the warmth before it would let the rest of the day in." She shook her head. "I took maybe sixty frames this morning, and I think one of them actually got it."

"Can I see?" Denny said.

"Sure. It's on the porch. Hang on." She pushed back from the table, went to the porch, and came back with the camera. She turned it on and scrolled to the frame and handed it to Denny.

He held it with both hands and a kind of reverence that she understood. He looked at it for a long time.

"That's incredible," he said.

"Let me see," Ruby said, leaning over.

Denny tilted the screen toward her and Ruby put her hand over her mouth the way people do when something catches them off guard.

"Bobby, that's the creek? Our creek?"

"Just past where the fence line crosses."

"I walk past there every week and I've never seen it look like that."

"You're not there at six in the morning," Judd said.

"I am absolutely there at six in the morning. I just don't have a fancy camera."

Bobby smiled. "The lens does most of the work."

Ruby passed the camera to Judd, who looked at it with his head tilted slightly, the way he looked at anything he was taking seriously. He nodded once and passed it down the table to Wyatt.

Bobby was talking to Ruby when, mid-sentence, her eyes swept the table and caught Wyatt's.

Despite having the camera in hand, his eyes were on her. His expression hadn't changed. It never changed. But his eyes were on her face and they stayed there for a full second before she looked away and picked up her sentence where she'd dropped it. But she lost the thread for a moment. By the time she found it again, her voice felt slightly different. She hoped no one would notice.

Wyatt looked down at the camera and studied the photo. Bobby couldn't help but steal glances from the corner of her eye as his gaze moved across the image and he took it in slowly, the way he took in everything.

He passed the camera to Denny.

"That's good," he said.

Two words. Then he picked up his fork and went back to his pot roast. Ruby glanced at Bobby, who had a look of small, quiet satisfaction on her face, like a woman watching a seed she'd planted start to break the soil.

AFTER SUPPER, the kitchen was cleared, Denny disappeared toward his room, Judd went out to the bunkhouse. Bobby stepped onto the porch to get her camera bag, and the night was so wide and warm that she stood taking it in for a moment.

The stars were out, thick and close, the way they'd been every night since she'd arrived, but somehow they seemed even clearer tonight. The scent of sweet grass rose with the last heat of the day, while the hint of a breeze moved the hair at her temples. From somewhere out in the dark pasture, a cow lowed once and was answered by another.

The screen door opened behind her, and Wyatt came out. He stopped when he saw her.

"Sorry," she said, and reached for her camera bag. "I was just grabbing this."

He nodded and stepped off the porch. He was heading for the barn. She watched him go for a second, and then she said it before she thought about it.

"Wyatt."

He turned.

"Thanks for the ride today. Into town."

He stood there in the yard, barely lit by the porch light. "You're welcome," he said. It was more than he usually gave, and he had to know it.

She sure did. As he walked toward the barn, she walked toward the bunkhouse. For about thirty yards, their paths ran together in parallel across the packed dirt of the yard. Their boots made soft sounds on the ground and, at some point, they fell into sync.

The barn loomed up on the left, dark against the sky. The bunkhouse was straight ahead, maybe forty yards farther. This was where their paths would split. Bobby slowed without meaning to, and Wyatt slowed too. They stood for a moment at the place where the yard divided.

The stars were enormous. The breeze carried the smell of the pasture and the faint sweetness of the wildflowers that had been blooming along the fence line all week. The ranch house behind them threw a yellow square of light from the kitchen window across the yard, and beyond that, everything was dark, open, and still.

Bobby looked at Wyatt. He was already looking at her, or maybe he'd just turned his head; she couldn't tell which. His face was mostly shadow, but she could see his eyes and, for the first time since she'd arrived, they weren't guarded. They were unlike anything she had seen from him or anyone else. They were just open, and looking at her directly. It felt like he could see through her. She went still.

Neither spoke. The breeze moved through the live oak by the barn, and the leaves made a dry, rushing sound that faded into the quiet. From somewhere south, a coyote called, thin and high, but wasn't answered.

"Night," he said.

"Good night," she replied.

He went left toward the barn, and she went straight to the bunkhouse. She didn't look back because she knew, if she did, something would break open that she wasn't prepared for. She had just over a week left here, a life in New York, and no business standing in a dark Texas yard feeling whatever it was she was feeling.

She went inside, closed the door behind her, and set down her bag on the floor. On the edge of the bunk, she sat pressing her palms flat on her thighs and looked at the window full of stars.

WYATT PUT the feed supplements he'd gotten in town on the shelf where they belonged. Then he stood in the barn with his hands on the stall door and listened to the horses shift and breathe in the dark.

After a minute, he went back to the porch, where he sat in his usual chair at the far end, the one where his father had sat all those years, and he put his boots on the rail. The night was warm, and the stars were doing what they always did, which was make everything else seem small and temporary. There he sat, looking out at the shadowy shapes of the ranch he'd been running since he was twenty.

He was tired. That was what he told himself. It had been a long day with a drive into town. He had a fence to check in the morning, and a list of more things that needed doing that was longer than one day could hold. But tomorrow, he'd get up at four-thirty and start over again, because that was what the ranch needed, and the ranch was what mattered.

Across the yard, the bunkhouse was a dark shape

against the horizon except for the window on the near side, where a warm yellow light shone through the darkness.

He sat there and looked at that light. He didn't think about the way she'd talked at dinner, her hands moving, and her face lit up in a way when she talked about the land. He didn't think about the way her eyes had caught his across the table, or the half second before she'd looked away. He didn't think about the walk across the yard, or the place where they'd stopped, and the starlight softened the night.

The light in the bunkhouse window went off.

A coyote called out again, closer now, and the horses were quiet in the barn. The ranch settled around him the way it did every night, familiar, enormous, and his.

He took his boots off the railing and went inside.

CHAPTER SIX

AT SUPPER, Ruby said, "Denny punched a boy at school."

Wyatt set his fork down. "He did what?"

"Punched him. Right in the face," Ruby said, as if reporting the weather, but her hands were busy with her napkin, folding and refolding the same corner. "A kid named Tyler grabbed Paloma Reyes's phone out of her hands at the lockers, held it over her head, and started going through her pictures and texts, and reading them out loud. What she'd texted, who she'd texted. The whole hall could hear."

Judd cut a piece of cornbread and said nothing.

"Paloma was close to tears. Denny told him to give it back. Tyler laughed. So Denny hit him." Ruby smoothed the napkin flat. "One punch. Broke the skin on his own knuckle. So he's got two days of detention starting tomorrow."

Wyatt looked at the empty chair where Denny usually sat. The boy was in his room. Whether he'd been sent there by Ruby or gone there on his own, Wyatt couldn't tell.

"How's his hand?"

"Swollen. I iced it. He'll be fine."

Wyatt picked his fork back up. He thought about what he would have done at fifteen if some kid had humiliated a girl in front of the whole school. He would have done exactly what Denny did, and his father would have felt exactly as he did right now: proud.

"Did you talk to him?" Wyatt asked.

"I told him violence isn't the answer. He said he knew. I told him there were consequences for acting like that. He said he knew it."

"Sounds like two days' detention is enough of a consequence."

"That's what I told him."

Bobby was quiet across the table. She'd glanced at Ruby a few times, but mostly studied her supper plate.

"Good for him," Judd said and went back to his cornbread.

THE PROBLEM SURFACED after the dishes were done.

Ruby was working the cast iron with a stiff brush. "So that's the end of tomorrow's plan," she said. "Denny was supposed to take Bobby out to the east range after school. Past the third gate, where the creek bends south. The cattle come down to the water late in the afternoon." She looked at Bobby. "You'd love it."

"It sounds beautiful," Bobby said.

"Denny wanted to show you the valley and maybe get some photography pointers while you shot." Ruby shook her head. "But by the time Judd picks him up from detention, the light'll be gone."

Bobby leaned against the counter. "I can go another day."

"You might run out of days." Ruby kept at the skillet. "Judd, you could take her."

Judd was drying a plate. He slowly set it on the stack while he shook his head, wincing. "My back's been at me since Monday."

"Your back?"

"My back. And my left hip. And that knee you told me to see a doctor about in January."

Ruby stared at him.

"I've been busy." Judd dried another plate.

"I'd go myself," Ruby said, "but somebody's gotta cook dinner." She set the skillet on the burner to dry and wiped her hands on the towel. Without looking at him, she said, "Wyatt, you'll be done with the north fence by early afternoon."

"I've got the vet call after that. Heifer's still limping."

"What time?"

Bobby stared at the floor.

Wyatt stood at the far end of the kitchen with his arms crossed. "Two."

"Perfect," Ruby said. "You'll be done by three, which leaves you time to ride out and get back before supper." Ruby smiled.

"Fine," he said, and left the kitchen before she could say anything else.

Behind him, he heard Bobby say, "Ruby, you didn't have to—"

"I know, but it's done," Ruby said. "Two o'clock."

HE HAD the horses ready by quarter to two, because if he was going to lose an afternoon to this, he was going to get the tack right and not waste a single minute more than necessary. He saddled Shadow, and then pulled Dolly's saddle off the rack and set it on her back. Dolly was sixteen years old, unflappable, and had the smoothest walk of any horse on the property. She'd carried beginners, children, and one very drunk Earl Dawson home from a poker game without incident. She'd be fine for a city gal who'd never been on a horse.

He was adjusting Dolly's cinch when Bobby came around the corner of the barn.

She was in her new ropers, the honey-brown ones she'd bought in Kerrville. Her jeans were tucked in. She had her camera bag slung across her body, and her hair was pulled back in a way that would fit under a hat if she'd had one, which she didn't. The afternoon was warm and bright, with the sky a hard blue that the Hill Country did better than anywhere he'd ever been, which admittedly wasn't many places.

"You ever been on a horse?" he said.

"A few times."

He looked at her. A few times could mean anything from a pony ride at a county fair to a dude ranch vacation where they walked you around a paddock and called it a trail ride. He pulled Dolly forward.

"This is Dolly. She's patient. When you mount, grab the horn with your left hand, put your left foot in the stirrup, and swing your right leg over. Don't kick her. She doesn't need it. A little pressure with your calves and she'll walk. Pull left to go left, right to go right, and back gently to stop. I'll go over the rest once you're settled."

Bobby walked to Dolly's left side, stood at her shoulder, and gathered the reins in her left hand. She put her left foot in the stirrup, pushed off the ground, and swung up in one clean motion. Her seat was centered. Her heels dropped. She adjusted the reins with both hands, found her balance, and looked down at him.

"My grandparents had a horse farm in Dutchess County, NY," she said. "I spent my summers there until I was eleven. It's been a while, but I remember the basics."

She said it plainly and sat that horse like the muscle memory had been waiting for her and she'd simply called it back for the occasion.

Wyatt stood there with one hand on Dolly's bridle, and the lecture he'd prepared suddenly had nowhere to go. He looked at her boots in the stirrups, her hands quiet on the reins, the easy line of her spine. This woman from New York City sat a horse like she'd been born to it. He hadn't expected that, but he kept not expecting things from her, and then she would surprise him, like a door he thought was shut swinging open without sound.

"All right then," he said. He let go of the bridle, mounted Shadow, and turned toward the east gate.

THEY RODE OUT AT A WALK, side by side where the trail was wide enough, single file through the cedar breaks. The afternoon heat had eased off its midday worst, and the air smelled like the dry sage-green grass that grew in tufts all around them. The Hill Country in the afternoon was a different place than the Hill Country at dawn. The colors were bolder. The live oaks threw long pools of shade across the trail, and where the sun hit the native grass full on, it turned from sage to a bleached gold that ran all the way to the ridge.

Bobby hadn't said a word since they left the barn, but she was looking at everything.

He watched her from the corner of his eye. She rode well, but rusty in small ways. He could see a slight stiffness in her hips that would work itself out in twenty minutes. Her hands were a little high on the reins, but her instinct was right. She moved with Dolly instead of against her, and she wasn't gripping with her knees the way most beginners did. When the trail narrowed through a stand of cedar and the branches closed in overhead, she ducked and adjusted her weight without being told.

They cleared the third gate, and the valley opened below them. The creek ran through the low ground in a slow curve. The water was dark where it pooled and bright where it ran shallow over limestone. On the far bank, maybe forty head of cattle had come down to the water, spread along the creek in loose groups, some drinking, and others grazing in the shade of the cypress. The sun was angling from the west now, and the light came through the trees in long shafts that hit the water and broke apart on the surface.

Bobby reined Dolly to a stop. She didn't say anything for several seconds.

"Oh," she said.

He'd seen this valley a thousand times. He'd ridden through it in every season and in every kind of weather since he was old enough to sit a saddle. He knew every bend in that creek, every rock, and every low spot that flooded in the spring. He knew where the cattle liked to stand, where the herons fished in the shallows, and where the cypress roots made a tangle at the water's edge.

He'd stopped seeing any of it. Somewhere in the last few years, between the bank calls, the feed bills, the Argentine import quotas, and the slow shrinking of everything his family had built, the valley had become a line item. Acreage. Carrying capacity. A parcel he'd considered selling on the days when the numbers didn't work, which was most days.

Bobby pulled her camera from the bag. Her hands were quick and sure. She checked the settings, lifted it to her eye, and the shutter clicked once. It was the only sound in the valley besides the water and the cattle and a dove calling from somewhere in the cypress.

She swung her right leg over the saddle to dismount, and her left boot caught in the stirrup.

The new leather was stiff. The heel had settled into the curve of the iron during the ride, and when she shifted her weight to step down, it didn't release. She was half off with one hand on the cantle and one foot in the air, nothing under her, and Dolly shifted.

"Hang on." Wyatt was off Shadow before he'd finished the sentence.

He put one hand on Dolly's neck to steady her and the other on Bobby's waist. She was laughing.

"It's the new leather," she said. "I should have broken them in."

"Hold still." He reached down with his free hand and worked the heel. A quarter turn and the boot slid loose from the iron. "There. Come on."

She came down. His hand was still on her waist, and she slid against him on the way, shoulder blade to chest, the whole length of her back against the whole length of his front because there was nowhere else for her to go. He was standing too close. Her boots hit the ground, her weight settled, and she was leaning against him, her head just below his jaw, and he breathed in the scent of her hair.

She turned her head and looked up at him. His eyes met hers, then swept over the freckles across her nose, the soft wisps of hair on her forehead, and back to the flecks of green in her brown eyes. She was half-smiling when the smile faded. He recognized the expression because he was sure his was the same: stunned with nothing to say about any of it.

The warm air was still around them, and his hand was still on her waist.

He let go. She stepped forward. The distance came back, and neither mentioned that moment.

Bobby turned away, dropped Dolly's reins to

ground-tie her, and walked toward the creek bank with the camera already at her eye. She moved fast, picking her way over the limestone with her shoulders set and her focus locked on the next frame, and Wyatt stood where she'd left him with his hand still feeling the shape of her.

He got back on Shadow, gathered the reins, and told himself to ride the fence line along the south side while she worked. Check the posts. Do something useful. That was the plan, and it was a good plan, but he sat there on Shadow and didn't move.

She crouched low by the water's edge and shot upstream where the light came through the cypress canopy. She stood, walked twenty yards, and framed the cattle against the far ridge, the long slope of grass behind them running up to a sky that was going deep blue in the hour before sunset. She lay flat on her stomach in the grass to get below the line of a calf drinking at the water's edge, and the camera clicked three times fast.

In the midst of the valley he'd known and loved all his life, there she was.

The late afternoon sun dropped low enough to come in sideways through the cypress and turn everything warm. He'd been too busy to ride out here in months. Bobby was reminding him of it without trying, just by the way she moved through his land with that camera, the way she stopped, crouched, and tilted her head at an angle of light he'd walked past a hundred times. The valley was coming back to life as the place his grandfather had ridden, where his father had sat a horse and probably felt the same thing Wyatt was feeling now, which was too large and too deep in his soul.

But that wasn't all of it. That was the easy, safe part, a man seeing his land through fresh eyes. The other part was trouble, and he'd known it since she slid down the front of him and neither of them stepped away fast enough.

He watched her rise from the grass with her knees dusty and her hair coming loose from its tie, and he watched her push it back from her face with one hand while the other held the camera steady. And that's when he knew. The way a man knows weather, the temperament of a horse, or the exact moment a fence line gives. He knew it in his body before his mind could catch up. This wasn't a woman he could stand next to and feel nothing, although that's what he'd been telling himself since he met her. She was just passing through. That was true. But it wasn't the whole truth. The whole truth was standing in his valley with creek mud on her boots, and he simply could not look away.

It bothered him. It ought to have bothered him enough to stop looking at her, but it didn't.

Bobby worked for the better part of an hour. Wyatt should have been restless. He had a list as long as his arm of things that wouldn't get done today. Instead, he sat on Shadow with his hands loose on the horn and watched a woman from New York lie in the grass of his family's land to photograph a calf drinking water, and the list didn't matter. The fence line didn't matter. Nothing mattered except her, the valley, and the afternoon sun on her hair.

When Bobby was done, she slung the camera bag across her chest and walked back to Dolly. She gathered the reins and put her left foot in the stirrup, and this time she worked the heel in deliberately, seating it firmly before she pushed up. She swung over clean, settled into the saddle, and didn't look at Wyatt.

He turned Shadow toward home.

Bobby held the reins with steady hands and followed Wyatt's horse through the cedar break while she tried to forget the touch of his hand on her waist. She watched the trail, the low branches, and the way the light had changed in the hour they'd been in the valley. The sun was dropping lower, turning everything amber, but all she could think about was the feel of his chest against her back.

On the ride out, they'd been two people who didn't know each other well enough to fill an hour of silence. On the ride back, they were two people who knew each other too well to try.

He was ahead of her on the trail, his back straight, his hat low against the sun that was dropping toward the western hills. She watched the way he sat the horse, the economy of it, the way his body moved with the animal with no apparent effort. She'd seen men ride before, but this was different. He rode the way he did everything, as though it was simply part of how he existed in the world, confident and yet unpretentious.

The trail widened where it met the ranch road, and she brought Dolly up beside him. They rode the last quarter mile in parallel, the way they'd started, and the only sounds were the horses' hooves on the packed earth and a mockingbird somewhere in the live oaks.

At the barn, Wyatt took the horses. Bobby offered to help untack, but he said he had it. As she handed him Dolly's reins, their fingers touched. It was a brief, accidental contact that neither acknowledged, but which Bobby felt from her hand all the way to the base of her throat.

"Thank you," she said. "For this afternoon. I got some good shots."

He nodded. "Glad it worked out." He was looking directly at her with a gaze that was steady and direct, as if the walls she'd grown accustomed to navigating had come down.

"See you at supper," she said.

"Yes, ma'am."

She turned and walked toward the bunkhouse, suppressing a smile. *Yes ma'am.* Her boots made a steady sound on the packed dirt of the yard, and the late sun threw her shadow long across the ground ahead of her, and she kept walking because if she stopped, she would turn around, and if she turned around, she would see his face, and she wasn't ready for that.

She went inside. She closed the door and leaned on it. She let the camera bag slide to the floor, then she sat on the edge of the bunk, gripping the bedding and hoping her heart would stop pounding.

The room was quiet. Through the window, the light had gone the color of honey. She could hear the horses in the barn, Judd's truck pulling up in the yard, and Denny's voice as he got out. Somewhere far off, a red-tailed hawk was calling.

She stared at the window and thought about his hands on her waist—strong, sure, and warm. He'd held her for two seconds longer than he had to, and those two seconds were long enough for her to know that she was in trouble. The sudden release that followed told her everything about what those seconds had cost him.

She went to the window. She couldn't help herself. From somewhere near the barn, Wyatt spoke low to the horses as he unsaddled them. Bobby closed her eyes and listened until his voice was gone.

CHAPTER SEVEN

THE KITCHEN WAS warm and floury when Bobby came in that morning and found Ruby making kolaches. Ruby had the dough rolled out on the big wooden board, and a plate of sausage links waiting by the stove. The whole room smelled like yeast, butter, and beef fat. The radio on the windowsill was playing something with a fiddle, turned low.

"Mind if I watch?"

"Oh, you can do better than that," Ruby said. "Wash your hands, and I'll show you how to wrap them."

Ruby showed Bobby how to flatten a piece of dough into an oval, set a sausage link at one end, and roll the dough around it, pinching the seam and tucking the ends so the whole thing held together. It was simple in theory but not easy in practice. Bobby's first two split open at the seam. Her third held. Without looking up, Ruby said, "There you go."

They worked side by side at the counter. The

kitchen window was open, and the breeze that came through carried the sounds of the ranch: a gate latch, the low call of a cow somewhere past the barn, and the crunch of boots on gravel as Denny crossed the yard on his way to do his morning chores.

"Wyatt's grandfather built this house," Ruby said. She said it the way she said most things about the ranch, like she was talking about the weather, factual and easy. "Well, the bones of it. The kitchen was a porch back then. Pop enclosed it when I was little. He said Grandpa Cavanaugh would have rolled over in his grave at the idea of an indoor kitchen taking up that much good porch space, not to mention the heat."

Bobby smiled. "Was he right?"

"Probably. Grandpa was an outdoor person. He built the line shack up in the north pasture with his own hands when he was younger than Wyatt is now. He ran cattle up there for weeks at a time, just him and two dogs and whatever he could carry on a horse." Ruby set a sausage link on a piece of dough and rolled it tight. "Pop was different. Quieter. He ran the ranch the same way, but he did it from this kitchen table. Every evening, when the day's work was done, he'd sit right there with a beer and his ledger, going over the numbers before he turned in."

"And your mom?"

Ruby's hands didn't stop, but they slowed. "Mom died when I was fifteen. Wyatt was eighteen, Cole was seventeen, Heath was seven." She pinched a seam shut. "Fire ants. She was out in the south pasture checking on a calf and stepped on a mound. She didn't know she was allergic. None of us did. By the time

Pop got her to the truck and got the truck to the highway, it was too late."

Bobby set down the piece of dough she was holding. "Ruby."

"It was fast," Ruby said. Her voice was steady, the words worn smooth from telling. "That's what they told us. That it was fast, and she didn't suffer. I don't know if that's true, but it's what Pop needed to hear, so we all agreed to believe it."

She rolled another kolache, tight and even, and set it on the tray. "After that, it was me and Pop running the house. Well, me. Pop ran the ranch. I did the cooking, the cleaning, the school lunches, making sure Heath got to bed on time. I was fifteen."

She said it without self-pity, the way she said everything. Bobby understood now why Ruby moved through that kitchen the way she did, like the room belonged to her in a way that went deeper than habit. She'd earned it. She'd been cooking in this kitchen since she was a girl, because it had to be done.

"Three years later, Pop had his heart attack. Right there." Ruby nodded at the kitchen table. "Same chair he sat in every night."

Bobby already knew the rest. Judd had told her on the porch one evening, in his spare, unhurried way. Wyatt was twenty, two years into his degree at UT when it happened. He drove home, and the door closed behind him on everything he'd been building in Austin. But Ruby's version wasn't the same. Judd had told it like history. Ruby told it like someone who'd lived it.

"I was seventeen," Ruby said. She wasn't looking

at Bobby. "A junior in high school. Wyatt drove down from Austin that same night. By the end of the week, he'd withdrawn from his classes and broken his lease." She pinched a seam shut. "He never talked about going back. Not once."

"Cole stayed about a year," she said. "Long enough to know Wyatt had it covered. Then the rodeo circuit. He was good, and he knew it, and I think he needed to be somewhere that wasn't here." She paused. "Heath was nine. He barely remembers Mom. He was too young to understand what was happening with Pop. By the time he was old enough to ask questions, the answers had become the kind of thing nobody talked about anymore."

Bobby didn't ask why Wyatt had left Austin with a half-finished degree and a lease with two months still on it. There must have been some other way. But there was a shape in Ruby's telling, a careful gap around that part of the story, and Bobby let it stay. The missing piece wasn't Ruby's to give away.

Ruby slid the tray of kolaches toward the oven. "It's mostly him. Judd does what he can. Diego comes over from the Gonzalez place a few days a week and helps out some. But the weight of it, that's on Wyatt."

She opened the oven door, and the heat rolled out into the kitchen in a wave. Bobby stepped back. Ruby slid the tray in, closed the door, and wiped her hands on her apron. For a second she stood there, looking at the oven with an expression Bobby couldn't read—pride, maybe, or worry, or the particular helplessness of loving someone who's carrying more than they should and refusing to set any of it down.

"He's good at it," Ruby said. "He was born for it, the way Pop was." She turned back to the counter and began cleaning up the flour. "He just got handed a version of it that's harder than it should be."

The kolaches came out of the oven golden and steaming. Bobby burned the roof of her mouth on the first one and didn't care. They were extraordinary. The dough was soft and slightly sweet, the sausage inside was peppery and rich, and the combination was so good that she reached for a second before she'd finished chewing the first.

"Ruby, these are incredible."

"They're just kolaches."

"They're not *just* kolaches." Bobby set the second one down and looked at Ruby. The photographer in her brain, the part that was always framing and composing, did the thing it did when it saw something worth paying attention to. "How many of these can you make in a day?"

Ruby gave her a look. "How many can you eat?"

"I'm serious. You've got these, you've got Judd's brisket, you've got that jalapeño cornbread you made Tuesday."

"That's just cornbread with peppers."

"It's a recipe. Your recipe. And the baked beans. And pecan pie."

"Oh, the beans are Judd's. Don't let him hear you giving me credit." Her eyes twinkled.

Bobby wiped her hands on a dish towel and leaned against the counter. "Ruby, you could sell these. All of it. A subscription box, direct from the ranch. Cavanaugh Creek grass fed beef, Ruby's kolaches, a cornbread mix, baked beans, pecan pie. Everything smoked, baked, or made right here on the ranch."

Ruby was quiet for a second. "I've thought of just selling the beef. But my cooking?" She was holding a kolache in one hand and a dish towel in the other, and Bobby could see her working through it, as if testing it in her practical way, looking for the place where it could all fall apart.

"Who would buy it?"

"Everyone. Anyone who reads the magazine piece and falls in love with this place. Anyone who wants a taste of real down-home cooking without all the corn syrup and chemicals they pack into everything else." Bobby picked up the kolache she'd set down. "I'd buy it, and I'm standing in the kitchen where they were made."

"We'd need packaging," Ruby said. "Labels. A website."

"All doable. And I'll ask Kay to put a link in the article." Bobby's brain raced with ideas. "You'd need graphics and photographs." Bobby looked at her. "Good ones. Food photography, product shots, the ranch in the background. The kind of pictures that make someone in Connecticut open their laptop and type in a credit card number."

Ruby looked at the tray of kolaches. She looked at Bobby. The corner of her mouth was doing a thing that Bobby recognized from a week of watching Ruby process information, a slow half-smile that meant she was taking something seriously.

"What exactly would go in the box?" Ruby said.

Bobby pulled a chair out from the kitchen table and

sat down. Ruby sat across from her. The kolaches steamed on the tray between them, and for the next hour they built it, piece by piece, item by item, until it went past a dream and began to feel real.

The brisket. Judd's brisket, smoked on the hand-built offset smoker his father had welded from a fifty-five-gallon drum. That was the anchor. You opened the box, and the brisket was the first thing you saw.

Next came Judd's baked beans, her kolaches, a jalapeño cornbread mix, and a pecan pie for dessert.

"The pecans come from the trees along the creek," Ruby said. "Pop planted those."

Bobby nodded, wheels turning. "And a photograph. A postcard-sized picture of the ranch, different every month. Denny could take them."

Ruby went still for a second, as though the idea had landed in a place she hadn't expected.

"Denny," she said.

"He's got a good eye. I've seen the way he looks at things." Bobby pulled out her phone and started making a list. "He takes the monthly photo, you put it in every box, and the subscribers feel like they know this place. Each person in the family contributes something so people aren't just buying food. They're buying a piece of ranch life."

Ruby sat back in her chair. She looked at the list on Bobby's phone, at the tray of kolaches on the table, at the kitchen where her father had sat every evening with his ledger and his beer. Bobby watched her face and saw the idea take hold, shifting from an impossible fantasy to a real, viable option.

"I'd need to talk to Wyatt," Ruby said.

"Of course."

"He'll say we can't afford it."

"Then we show him the numbers."

Ruby looked at her across the table, and there was an expression on her face that Bobby hadn't seen before—raw, unguarded hope. Perhaps it was the idea of being able to reach for a life she could choose instead of one she'd inherited.

"Ruby, we could do this."

"We," Ruby said.

Bobby hadn't meant to say it. The word had come out of its own accord, and she heard it the same moment Ruby did, and she understood what it meant. It wasn't just a suggestion from a visitor but an offer from someone who felt like part of the ranch.

Bobby added, "I mean I could help. I could take the pictures, help design the logo, the packaging, website—all of it. I would love to help you launch this."

Ruby reached across the table and squeezed her hand. She didn't say anything. She didn't need to.

Bobby called Kay from the porch of the bunkhouse at ten, still warm from the kitchen, the coffee, and the quiet certainty that a door had just opened.

"The assignment shots are done," Bobby said. "I filed them last night. You should have everything."

"I saw. They're gorgeous." Kay's voice had the clipped warmth of a woman who gave compliments the way she gave deadlines: fast and final. "The creek shot with the cattle. Bobby, that's a cover."

"I was hoping you'd say that."

"So you're heading back Saturday?"

Bobby looked out across the yard. Judd was walking toward the equipment shed with a coffee mug in one hand and a fence tool in the other. From somewhere behind the barn she could hear Wyatt's voice, deep and steady, talking to the horses. She'd gotten used to the sound of it. She'd gotten used to a lot of things she hadn't planned on.

"Actually," she said, "I'm going to stay on another week."

A pause. Kay's pauses were rare and therefore a little unsettling.

"Ruby, Wyatt's sister, has a business idea. A mail-order thing, direct-to-consumer beef and smoked meat from the ranch. She needs food photography for the packaging and the website. I told her I'd help."

"Way to hustle, Bobby."

"Oh, no. It's actually a personal project. I'm not charging her. I'm just helping out." Bobby kept her voice light, the way she did when she was steering a conversation away from the thing she didn't want to talk about. "It's like a vacation, Kay. When's the last time I took a vacation?"

"Twenty twenty-two. Tulum. You brought your camera, shot three rolls of medium format on the beach, and came back with a tan line from your camera strap."

"That counts."

"It does not count." Kay was quiet for a second. "Is the ranch nice, at least? Are you comfortable?"

"It's beautiful. The family's been really welcoming."

"The family."

"Ruby. Judd, the ranch hand. Ruby's son, Denny, he's fifteen, great kid."

She'd left out Wyatt's name. It just happened, and she knew Kay had noticed, but neither of them remarked on the omission. Bobby looked at the barn. The horse talk had stopped. The yard was empty and bright in the sun.

"All right," Kay said. "Enjoy your vacation. Send me a postcard."

Bobby smiled and rolled her eyes but said nothing.

"And Bobby?"

"Yeah."

"Enjoy your personal project. You deserve it."

Bobby caught Kay's innuendo, but before she could say anything, Kay had another call and cut their call short.

Bobby hung up and sat on the porch step. The morning was warm, and she still had the taste of kolache in her mouth. She sat there for a while, looking at the ranch and thinking about subscription boxes and Ruby's face when she'd said "we."

THAT AFTERNOON, Bobby helped Ruby wash the breakfast dishes. The brainstorming high had settled into something quieter, and the kitchen had the easy, unhurried feel of two women who'd spent enough time together to be comfortable in silence.

Bobby dried frying pan and set it in the drainer. She'd been thinking about it all morning, the thing Ruby hadn't said, the space in the family story that no one had filled in.

"Can I ask you something?" Bobby said. "And you can tell me it's none of my business."

"You can ask."

"Denny's father."

Ruby kept washing. Her hands moved at the same steady pace, and she didn't tense up or go quiet the way people did when you'd stumbled into a wound. She just washed.

"We were in the same grade, and went to prom senior year."

She rinsed a glass and set it in the drainer. "Pop had been gone for two years. Wyatt was trying to keep the ranch going. Cole was still around but he had one foot out the door. I'd been running that house since I was fifteen, and I was so tired of being the grown-up." She turned off the water. "Prom was the first night in three years that I felt like a kid."

She dried her hands on the towel and leaned against the counter, facing Bobby. "He was sweet. Kind of quiet, kind of funny. We'd been friends for a while and then it turned into something more, the way things do when you're eighteen, life is taking off, and everything suddenly feels bigger than it is. It lasted through the summer. Then he went off to college out east in August, and I knew by September."

"Did you tell him?"

"No." Ruby said it simply. "We both knew it wasn't going to last past the summer. I didn't see the point of turning his life upside down. I mean, what would it have accomplished? He would have tried to do the right thing, but it would have ruined his life. He would have resented me, and it couldn't have lasted. So what was the point? I was better off on my own."

Bobby set the dish towel on the counter. "That's a lot at eighteen."

"I had help. Wyatt asked who the father was, but I wouldn't tell him. He never asked again, not once." Ruby's eyes teared up. "If I didn't love him already, I would love him for that. He just asked, 'What do you need.'" Judd built the crib. Ruby smiled. "And in this house full of guys, they all got me through it. And then I had Denny and he was the best thing that ever happened to me or to this family. He came along right when we needed someone to be happy about."

She picked up the dish towel Bobby had set down and folded it over the oven handle.

Bobby looked at this woman who had buried her mother at fifteen, her father at seventeen, had a baby at nineteen, and built a life in a kitchen that had been hers since before she was old enough to drive. Ruby Cavanaugh had never once asked anyone to feel sorry for her, and Bobby understood that asking was not something she intended to start.

"So," Ruby said, and her voice shifted back to her usual brisk warmth. "About this subscription box. I think we need to talk to Wyatt about this."

THAT EVENING, Bobby sat on the bunk with her laptop balanced on her knees. She'd been meaning to do this since she filed the assignment photos with Kay. But there were more photos, the ones she'd taken for herself.

She opened a folder labeled "Ranch Misc" because she'd created it in a hurry on the third day and never renamed it, and it had grown without her paying much attention to how large it was getting.

She scrolled past the landscapes, past the equipment shots, and the detail work—the leather of a saddle horn worn smooth, a fence post with fifty years of barbed wire scars, and Denny's boots by the back door. She scrolled past all of that and arrived at the ones she'd been avoiding.

Six photos of Wyatt.

She had no memory of deciding to take most of them. That was the unsettling part. Bobby Tapley did not take accidental photographs. She had been shooting professionally for twelve years, and every frame she'd ever filed came from a conscious decision to press the shutter at a specific instant for a specific reason. She knew her own process, and she trusted it.

These were different.

The first was from the fence line on the fourth day. Wyatt was leaning on a post with his hat pushed back, squinting at something in the distance. The late afternoon light caught the side of his face in a way that turned his jaw sharp and his eyes pale. She must have lifted the camera and shot without thinking about it, the way you reach for a glass of water and take a drink.

The second was from the barn. He was carrying a saddle, one arm through the gullet, and he was half-turned toward the camera as if she'd said his name, though she didn't remember saying it. The expression on his face was unguarded in a way she'd never seen when he knew she was looking.

The third was from the kitchen. He was sitting at the table with a coffee mug in both hands, and Ruby was talking to him from the stove. He was listening with his head tilted slightly, looking patient and unhurried, as if there were no question about it. His sister deserved his full attention.

She scrolled slowly and looked at the fourth, fifth, and sixth. Part of her looked at each one the way she looked at contact sheets in the studio, evaluating the technical choices she'd made. But the other part studied the man.

They were good. That was the problem. They weren't just well-lit candids of a photogenic man. These had intimacy in them in the way they revealed an unguarded side of the man. But they also revealed how she felt about him.

Bobby closed the laptop. The room was dim now except for the thin line of light under the door and the last light of sunset coming through the window. She could hear the ranch settling into evening. Ruby called Denny in from the yard. The screen door closed. A cow mooed from somewhere beyond the barn.

She opened the laptop again. The six photographs were still there, still arranged in a neat row, still looking back at her with all the things she hadn't meant to notice.

She didn't delete them.

She closed the laptop for good this time, with her hands flat on the lid and the screen's warmth fading under her palms. Through the window, she could hear the faint sounds of the kitchen—silverware, Ruby's laugh, Denny's voice going on about something. It was time to go in for supper. She would, in a minute.

She sat there a little longer and thought about a man carrying a saddle with the sun on his face and the way he'd looked when he didn't know she was watching. She pressed her palms flat on the laptop and didn't move.

CHAPTER EIGHT

ON FRIDAY EVENING, the ranch changed.

Bobby noticed it first in the barn. She'd come out after supper to shoot the last light on the equipment shed, and the barn doors were open wide, throwing a long rectangle of electric light across the yard. Inside, every surface was covered. Saddles on the racks, bridles hanging from hooks along the wall, ropes coiled on the fence rail in neat loops. Wyatt was at the far end checking a cinch strap, running it through his hands with focused attention. Diego was next to the stock trailer, loading gear, and Judd had stationed himself in a lawn chair just outside the doors with a bottle of Shiner in hand and opinions about everything.

"That headstall needs oiling," Judd said to no one in particular.

"Be my guest," Diego said with a smile teasing the corners of his mouth.

Bobby leaned on the fence and watched. The rodeo

was tomorrow. She'd gathered that from Ruby over the past two days, in pieces, from a mention at breakfast, a comment about the schedule, and Denny asking if he could borrow Wyatt's good rope. It was a local ranch rodeo, the kind communities all over Texas put on throughout the year. Wyatt roped. That was all Ruby had said about it, as if this were no more remarkable than the fact that he also fixed fences and fed cattle.

He'd gather the reins a fraction of an inch, and the horse would collect. She had never seen this from him before. He did everything on the ranch with quiet competence, but this was different. This was a man doing the thing he was born to do, and he knew it the way a musician knows a song he's played since childhood, in his hands, his spine, and the bottoms of his feet.

Bobby raised her camera. The shutter clicked once, then again, and then she lowered it and watched. The ropes on the fence rail, the cinch in his hands, the trailer hitched in the yard against the last color of the sky. She shot all of it. These weren't assignment photos. The assignment was filed and in Kay's inbox. These were for her. She kept shooting because stopping would mean admitting why she'd started.

Diego finished loading the trailer and walked to the barn to wipe down the saddles. He worked steadily and didn't talk much, which was normal for Diego. Bobby had been at the ranch for a week, and she could count on two hands the number of complete sentences she'd heard from him. He was about Ruby's age, maybe a year or two younger, with dark eyes and a build that suggested he'd been throwing hay bales since he could walk. He was good at his work. Wyatt trusted him, which, based on what Bobby had seen, was not a thing Wyatt gave away cheaply.

"Diego, you're staying for supper," Ruby said from the porch. It wasn't a question. "I made too much chicken-fried steak, and you're not going home hungry."

Diego looked at Ruby, and his hands went still on the saddle. A half-second hesitation, the briefest recalibration, as though Ruby's voice had come from a different direction than he'd expected, and he needed to find his footing.

"I appreciate that," he said. "Thank you, Ruby."

SUPPER WAS LOUD. Denny was excited about the rodeo and talked more than Bobby had heard from him all week. Ruby kept the conversation moving. Judd ate. Wyatt answered Denny's questions about the roping order with a patience Bobby hadn't seen from him before, and she filed that away too, the way she filed everything: Wyatt was different with Denny. Softer. She saw it in the spaces between his words, the half-second longer he held eye contact, and the way he listened when Denny talked about his event tomorrow as though a fifteen-year-old's junior team roping mattered as much as anything else on the schedule.

But it was Ruby who caught her interest that evening.

The table was loud. Denny was vibrating with

tomorrow's energy, talking about his roping partner and their strategy for the junior division. Judd was holding court about rodeos he'd seen over the decades, and Wyatt was answering Denny's questions with a patience Bobby hadn't expected. Even Diego joined in, telling Denny a story about the first time he'd missed a dally and the rope burned a stripe across his palm.

Ruby was unusually quiet.

That was what caught Bobby's attention. Ruby, who ran every conversation at this table, who drew people out and kept the rhythm going, was eating her chicken-fried steak and saying practically nothing. She smiled when Denny said something funny. She passed the biscuits when Judd pointed. But the woman who usually held this kitchen together with her voice was sitting across from Diego with her eyes on her plate and a flush along her cheekbones that the stove couldn't account for.

Every few minutes, she seemed to catch herself and say something like, "Denny, tell Bobby about the time you roped the fence post." For a sentence or two, she'd sound like regular Ruby. Then she'd go quiet again.

Diego was no better. He talked easily enough to Judd, Wyatt, and Denny, but when Ruby handed him the gravy boat, their fingers brushed, and he thanked her without looking up. Bobby read body language for a living. She knew what two people looked like when they were aware of each other, and these two were acutely aware of each other.

Bobby understood that feeling too well. She looked

down at her plate and thought about the six photographs of Wyatt on her laptop.

After supper, Bobby helped Ruby dry the dishes while the men dispersed to their various corners of the ranch. The kitchen was warm, the window was open, and the smell of fried steak lingered in the air.

Bobby kept her voice casual. "Diego seems nice."

Ruby's hands kept moving on the plate she was washing. "He is nice. He's been coming around here since we were kids."

"You grew up together?"

"His family's ranch is the next property over. He was a couple of years behind me in school," Ruby said it evenly, the way you'd describe a neighbor, a fact of geography. But her hands had slowed on the plate.

Bobby dried a glass and set it on the shelf. "He was pretty chatty at supper tonight. With Denny and Judd, anyway."

Ruby didn't answer right away. She rinsed the plate, set it in the drainer, and reached for the next one.

"You were quiet," Bobby said.

"Was I?" Ruby said. "I was tired. Long day."

Bobby recognized the deflection because she'd been making the same one about Wyatt for a week. She let it go.

"He's got good hands," Bobby said. "With the tack."

Ruby turned off the water. "He does," she said, dried her hands on the towel, and that was the end of it.

Saturday morning came up bright and warm, and by nine o'clock, they were all in Wyatt's truck heading south on Route 16. Ruby had packed a cooler. Denny had his rope in the truck bed. Diego followed in his own truck with the stock trailer. Bobby sat in the back seat next to Denny with her camera bag between her feet and watched the Hill Country roll past in the morning light, the limestone bluffs, the live oaks, and the wildflowers along the shoulder in drifts of blue, red, and yellow.

The rodeo grounds were south of town, a dirt arena with metal bleachers and a series of corrals and holding pens behind the chutes. When they pulled in, the lot was already half full of pickups and stock trailers. Bobby could smell livestock, dust, and fried food from the concession stand, and somewhere a loudspeaker was playing country music at a volume that suggested the day had started without them.

She climbed out and stood in the lot, taking it in. The grand entry was forming at the far end of the arena, riders on horseback carrying flags. Kids in hats too big for their heads ran between the trailers. A woman in a lawn chair by the gate had a baby on one hip and a program in the other hand. Two old men leaned on the rail and watched the warm-up pen, where a half-dozen riders circled at a jog, and said things to each other Bobby couldn't hear.

Wyatt was already at the trailer, helping Diego unload the horses. He'd changed out of his work clothes and into a clean pearl-snap shirt and a pair of dark Wranglers with a crease, and his good hat—the black felt one Bobby had only seen on the hook by the door. He looked like a different man. Not different, exactly. He looked like the same man in sharper focus.

Ruby appeared at Bobby's elbow. "You'll want to be in the stands for team roping," she said. "Right side, down low. You can see the box from there."

"The box?"

"Where the ropers back their horses in before the run. Trust me. That's where you want your camera pointed."

Bobby nodded, slung her bag over her shoulder, and made her way through the crowd to the bleachers. She found a spot on the right side, three rows up, and settled in with her long lens.

The grand entry started at 8:30. Riders came through the gate single file, carrying the American flag, the Texas flag, and the arena flag. The crowd stood, and the announcer's voice came through the speakers, tinny and warm, welcoming everybody to the annual Hill Country Ranch Rodeo. The cheering was big enough to tell Bobby that everyone here knew everyone else and had been coming to this thing for years.

She shot the flags, the dust rising in the morning sun, the line of riders, and a little girl on a paint horse who couldn't have been more than eight and who sat that saddle like it was her destiny.

The morning events ran in blocks: bareback broncs first, then saddle bronc, then tie-down roping. Bobby shot all of it, but she was waiting for team roping, and when the announcer called it, she leaned forward and put her eye to the viewfinder.

Wyatt was in the third pair. His partner was a man Bobby didn't recognize. He was older, lean, with a dark mustache and the unhurried assurance of someone who'd done this a thousand times. They backed their horses into the boxes on either side of the chute, and when the steer broke, they went.

It was fast. Bobby had photographed horse races, polo matches, and all kinds of athletic events where speed was the point, but this was different. There was no wasted motion. Wyatt's loop went out flat and clean and settled over the horns, and he dallied and turned the steer in one movement, and his partner was already off the mark, the heel loop sailing low and catching both hind legs, and the flag dropped. The crowd cheered. Bobby looked at her camera's timer. Under seven seconds.

She watched Wyatt rein his horse back, coil his rope with one hand, and lean over to say something to his partner. She watched the easy way people around her in the stands nodded and clapped, some even saying his name. He was among his people. The guarded, spare, careful man she'd been living alongside for a week was someone else here. He moved through the crowd behind the chutes with his rope over his shoulder, stopping to talk to three different people on his way back. Each time, his posture was easy and open, his face unhurried. He belonged here. It was as if the whole arena was an extension of his land. These were his neighbors. He didn't have to explain himself to any of them.

Bobby lowered her camera and looked at him across the distance of the arena.

THE YOUTH EVENTS came in the mid-afternoon, after the lunch break, when the sun was high and the shadows had pulled in close to the fences. After shooting all morning, Bobby's shoulders ached, and her water bottle was empty. She found a spot along the rail near the warm-up pen, where the junior ropers were getting ready.

Denny was in the third pair, the same as his uncle's. He'd borrowed Wyatt's second rope and was mounted on a bay that Diego had trailered over from the Gonzalez place. Bobby watched him warm up. He sat the horse the way Wyatt sat one, with that same still center, the same economy. He wasn't as smooth yet. His loop needed another year or two. But the bones were there, the same easy competence she'd watched all morning in the adult events, handed down through the family like the shape of a jawline or the color of their eyes.

She lifted her camera and followed him through the viewfinder as the steer broke and Denny went. His loop caught the horns on the first throw. He dallied hard, turned the steer, and held it while his partner threw for the heels. The crowd clapped. When he came out of the box, Denny's face had the controlled expression of a boy trying very hard not to grin.

Bobby tracked him through the lens as he rode toward the fence and stopped. That's when she saw it.

He wasn't looking at the timer board, his partner, or his uncle. He was looking at the stands.

Bobby followed his gaze. Third row, just left of center. A dark-haired girl about Denny's age sat with a woman who looked like her mother and a younger boy who was fidgeting with a snow cone. The girl was watching Denny with a still focus. Her hands were folded in her lap. Her chin was level. Her eyes didn't move from the boy on the horse.

Neither of them waved or looked away fast enough.

Bobby lowered her camera. This photograph wasn't hers to take.

THE AFTERNOON WORE ON. Bobby found a seat in the stands again and watched the last of the championship rounds and the awards ceremony. Wyatt and his partner placed second in team roping. Denny's pair came third in the junior division. The crowd thinned as the shadows lengthened, and the arena took on the amber cast of late afternoon in the Hill Country, the same light Bobby had been chasing with her camera since she'd arrived—warm, slanted, and generous.

She was sitting in the bleachers when Wyatt came through the gate below her with his hat pushed back on his head. He looked up and found her in the stands as though he'd known where she was sitting all along.

He didn't smile. He didn't wave. He just looked at her for a second, and then he turned and kept walking. It was nothing. A glance across a crowded arena. A man looking for his family and finding the photographer first.

But Bobby sat very still and watched him go, knowing that it wasn't nothing. It hadn't been nothing all day. Every time she'd caught herself looking at him, he'd been watching her. The whole afternoon had been an accumulation, a slow gathering of glances and near-misses that neither seemed able to stop.

The sun dropped lower, and the arena emptied. Bobby gathered her camera bag and climbed down from the bleachers. She found the truck, where Ruby was loading the cooler and Denny was telling Diego about his run in the kind of breathless detail that only a fifteen-year-old could sustain. Wyatt was at the trailer, checking the tie-downs on the horses, and when Bobby walked past, she was close enough to see the dust on his shirt, the sweat line on his hatband, and the way his hands moved on the rope. She kept walking because there was nothing to say that wouldn't have felt like too much.

Ruby looked at her as she climbed into the back seat. "Good day?" Ruby asked.

"Great day," Bobby said. She set her camera bag on the floor, buckled in, and looked straight ahead. "Really great day."

Ruby studied her for a second, said nothing, and smiled.

CHAPTER NINE

JUDD SAID, "GO."

It wasn't a suggestion, just the one word, delivered from his lawn chair by the stock trailer while Wyatt coiled ropes and tried to talk himself into a quiet night on the porch.

"Ruby's already got her mind set on it," Judd added. "You think you're going to win that one?"

He did not think he was going to win that one. Ruby had mentioned the Broken Spoke twice during the drive home from the rodeo, and the second time she'd looked at Bobby in the rearview mirror and said, "They've got a live band on Saturdays," and Bobby had said, "I'm in," and that was that. Ruby didn't need his permission. She didn't need him at all, technically. But she needed his truck. His truck meant him, and Judd knew it. Which was why Judd was sitting in his lawn chair with a Shiner in his hand and a look on his face that Wyatt had been seeing for thirty-two years.

"Fine," Wyatt said.

"Wear the good shirt," Judd said.

Wyatt didn't respond.

THE BROKEN SPOKE sat on a county road three miles south of town, a long limestone building with a corrugated metal roof and a gravel lot that was already full when they pulled in at eight thirty. Neon beer signs in the windows, a wooden porch along the front, and the bass line of a country band thumping through the walls and into the parking lot like a second heartbeat.

Wyatt cut the engine and sat for a second with his hands on the wheel.

Bobby was in the back seat. She'd changed out of her rodeo clothes and into a dark blue top he hadn't seen before, jeans, and her ropers. She'd done something with her hair that left it loose around her shoulders. He'd noticed when she climbed into the truck. He'd been noticing things about Bobby Tapley for nine days now, and it was just getting worse.

Ruby was already out of the cab when Denny climbed down from the truck bed where he'd been sitting with the cooler. Wyatt watched the boy straighten his hat and glance toward the front door with a look that was trying very hard to seem casual.

"You expecting somebody?" Wyatt asked.

Denny's ears went red. "No, sir."

Wyatt let it go. They walked in together, Ruby leading, Bobby beside her, and Wyatt trailing with Denny. Inside, the room was loud and warm and full of people he'd known his entire life. The band was on a low stage at the far end, a four-piece playing something by George Strait, and the dance floor was already moving. The bar ran along the left wall, scratched oak under yellow light, and every other stool was taken.

He scanned the room the way he always did, accounting for who was there and where. Tommy Hale and his wife by the bar. Two of the Urbanek brothers from the ranch supply. A cluster of young guys he recognized from the rodeo circuit near the pool table in the back. Diego was at the far end of the bar with a beer in front of him, sitting the way Diego sat everywhere: quiet, watchful, taking up less space than a man his size ought to.

Denny made his own scan. Quick, the whole room in two seconds, and then his shoulders settled a fraction of an inch. He said something to Ruby about getting a Coke. Wyatt knew the look. Whoever he'd been looking for wasn't here. He'd worn that look himself at fifteen, though he wouldn't have admitted that then and didn't plan to now.

"Go on," Wyatt told him. "Stay where we can see you."

Denny disappeared into the crowd with the typical speed of a teenager released from adult supervision.

Wyatt found a spot at the bar and ordered a beer. Tommy Hale leaned over and said something about the roping that afternoon, and Wyatt fell into the conversation the way he fell into all conversations with people he'd grown up with: easy, unhurried, his body angled toward Tommy and his eyes on the room.

He didn't watch Bobby, but he was aware of where

she was, which was a different thing and a distinction he was making for his own benefit.

Ruby had her by the wrist and was pulling her toward the dance floor. The band had shifted into something faster, a shuffle beat with a steel guitar that the older couples knew by heart, and Ruby was already moving. She said something to Bobby that Wyatt couldn't hear, and Bobby laughed, shook her head, and went, anyway.

"Your girl new in town?" Tommy said, as if he didn't know everyone in their town.

Wyatt looked at him. "She's not my girl."

Tommy drank his beer and didn't argue, which was the polite Texas version of completely disagreeing.

On the floor, Ruby walked Bobby through a line dance. Bobby was a half beat behind and going the wrong direction. She obviously knew it and was laughing so hard her whole face had changed. He'd seen her focused, he'd seen her quiet, and he'd seen her in control of her camera. He had never seen her like this. She was lit up. The blue top fluttered when she moved, and her hair swung across her shoulders as she turned left when everyone else turned right. Once, she nearly collided with a woman twice her size who caught Bobby by the elbow and set her straight without missing a step.

Ruby was patient and ruthless at the same time. She'd back up three counts and walk Bobby through the sequence with her hands on Bobby's hips, steering her, and Bobby would get it for eight bars and then lose it again. Ruby would grab her arm, and they'd both be laughing. The women on the surrounding floor were as generous as they were amused.

Bobby caught on faster than Wyatt expected. By the second song, she had the basic pattern and was beginning to keep up. She wasn't smooth; she lacked the muscle memory that came from growing up with these dances. But she was game, she was paying attention, and by the third song, she nearly fit in. Her hips loosened. Her weight shifted earlier. She was still behind, but she was behind in the right direction.

Tommy was talking about the price of hay. Wyatt said something in response that may or may not have been relevant.

He noticed Diego watching the floor. Diego had his beer in front of him and his back to the bar. He was doing what Wyatt had been doing, watching the whole floor while his eyes kept straying to a specific person. Wyatt couldn't help himself.

For Diego, the whole floor just happened to include Ruby, who was now two-stepping with Denny. His expression didn't change. That was what gave him away. A man with no stake in the matter would have looked elsewhere by now.

The song ended. Denny grinned and went back to his friends. Ruby fanned herself with one hand and said something to Bobby. They both came off the floor and headed for the bar. Bobby's cheeks were flushed and her eyes were bright. She was still breathing hard from the dancing when she passed Wyatt on her way to get water and grinned at him without stopping. That grin did more damage than anything that had happened between them all day.

The band changed tempo. A steel guitar started a slow melody, and the singer leaned into the mic and began the opening bars of a ballad that turned into a two-step. Couples moved onto the floor in pairs. The lighting changed, or maybe it hadn't, but the room felt different.

Wyatt looked at Diego. Diego was looking at his beer.

"Ruby likes this song," Wyatt said. He didn't look at Diego when he said it. He said it to the bar, to the air, to no one in particular, the same way Judd had said "Go" earlier that evening.

Diego went still. His hands tightened on the beer bottle, a small motion, barely visible. Then he set it down and stood up from the stool. He didn't say anything to Wyatt. He straightened his shirt and walked toward the end of the bar where Ruby was standing with a glass of water and her back to the dance floor.

Wyatt watched.

Diego said something. He said it quietly enough that Ruby had to lean in to hear, and in that lean Wyatt saw everything he needed to see. Her face. The easy, confident Ruby who ran the household and was unflappable, in one second, was caught completely off guard. Her lips parted, her eyes went wide, and she looked at Diego as though he'd said something in ancient Greek. She said something, set her water down on the bar, and took the hand that he'd offered.

They walked onto the floor. Diego put his hand on her waist and took her other hand, and they started to move. Whatever shyness had kept him on his stool for the last hour was gone the moment the music told him what to do. He could dance. Wyatt hadn't known that. Diego led Ruby through the two-step with a quiet authority that Wyatt recognized because it was the same thing he'd seen in Diego with a horse or a rope. Ruby followed him, and the surprise on her face gave way to a look Wyatt had never seen on his sister before.

He watched them for two passes around the floor and then took a sip of his beer. He didn't smile. He didn't look away, either. He just drank his beer and let the two of them have the floor.

"Well," Tommy Hale said.

Wyatt said nothing.

Bobby appeared at the bar. She'd gotten her water, found a stool two seats down from him, and she watched the dance floor with her chin in her hand. The flush from the line dancing had faded, and in its place was an expression he recognized. She was watching Ruby and Diego the way she watched everything, with an eye for detail. But underneath it, she was swaying. A small motion, barely there, her body keeping time with the music.

Her face in the bar light was open in a way it usually wasn't, to reveal a wistful softness in her eyes. She looked like a woman on the far side of a window.

He finished his beer. Tommy was talking to someone else now, and the band was still playing. Bobby swayed, and Wyatt watched her long enough to know that he didn't have a choice. He was past that. He'd been past it since the valley, since the caught stirrup, and since the moment in the arena that afternoon when he found her in the stands and couldn't pretend he'd been looking for anyone else.

He set his bottle on the bar and took a few steps to stand in front of her. She looked up.

He held out his hand. "Ma'am, may I have this dance?"

Her lips parted, but no answer came out. She looked at his hand, and then lifted her eyes to meet his, and whatever she saw there made her go very still. He waited. The music kept playing, and the room kept moving. He stood there with his hand out and his whole body aware that he could not take this back.

She took his hand. Her fingers closed around his, and she slid off the stool.

He led her to the floor. His right hand found her waist, her left hand came to his shoulder, and they clasped free hands between them. She was close. Closer than the stirrup. He could feel the warmth of her through the thin fabric of her shirt. Her hand felt small in his, and her shoulder was tense under his palm.

"I don't know how to two-step," she said.

"I'll lead. You follow. Quick quick, slow slow. That's all there is."

She nodded. He stepped forward, and she stepped back, a fraction late, and he corrected the spacing by instinct. He tightened his hand on her waist to guide her, and she found the rhythm on the third bar. Quick quick, slow slow. Her feet seemed to figure it out before her head did. He felt the moment she stopped counting and started moving. The tension in her shoulder eased, her weight settled into the pattern, and by the middle of the first verse, she was following him.

He kept his eyes on the room, on the surrounding couples, and on the band—anywhere but at her. Her hair brushed his jaw when she turned her head, and the scent of her, clean and warm, nearly went to his head.

When she looked up at him, he looked into her eyes.

He stopped hearing the band, the loud voices, or the clinking of glasses. For Wyatt, all that mattered was the space between her face and his. Her eyes were brown with those flecks of green that he'd noticed in the valley. She was simply looking at him, and he was looking at her, and the two-step kept them moving so neither of them had to decide what to do about it.

By the second verse, she'd relaxed into his lead, and her body was doing what it should have been doing all along, which was moving with his. As he turned and she followed, her hand tightened on his shoulder for balance. For one step, she was against his chest. He felt the length of her, soft and warm, the way she exhaled against his collar. Then she was back at a distance, and he missed her body against his.

When the last note held and faded, they stopped. His hand was still on her waist. Her hand was still on his shoulder. They stood on the dance floor and looked at each other while the crowd clapped and the band said something about taking five.

"Thank you," she said. Her voice was steady, but her hand was not.

He nodded. He let go of her waist. She let go of his

shoulder. They walked back to their separate seats at the bar.

WYATT DROVE THEM ALL HOME.

Ruby was in the front seat. Bobby was in the back with Denny, who had fallen asleep against the window before they hit the main road. The truck moved through the dark Hill Country roads.

Ruby looked out her window. Bobby looked out hers. Wyatt looked at the road and drove on.

No one spoke. The truck cab was filled with too many feelings and thoughts that would never be mentioned.

Wyatt pulled through the ranch gate and up the drive. The house was dark except for the porch light Ruby had left on and the light in Judd's bunkhouse window. He parked and cut the engine.

"Good night," Ruby said. She opened her door and shook Denny's shoulder, and the boy climbed out and followed her across the yard and into the house.

Bobby opened her door. "Good night, Wyatt."

"Night."

She climbed out, closed the door, and walked toward the bunkhouse. He watched her cross the yard in the porch light, her boots on the hard-packed dirt, her hair catching the light when she passed under the bulb by the barn door. She didn't look back.

After she'd gone inside, Wyatt sat on the porch in the chair his father and his grandfather before him had sat. The dark sky was big, and the stars were all out.

The ranch was quiet the way it always was at this hour, when the cattle had settled, the creek kept on running, and the wind whispered through the live oaks. He'd been hearing that sound his whole life, but tonight it wasn't enough.

He could still feel her hand in his, the shape of her waist against his palm, and the way she'd looked at him on the dance floor when the room faded away. He couldn't forget that unguarded expression, but what good would remembering do?

She was leaving in a week. He'd known that since the day she arrived, and it hadn't mattered until now. She had a life in New York City, a career in a world so far from these acres of Hill Country grass that there was no spanning the distance. There was no changing that.

But when she took his hand, and she looked in his eyes, he forgot. All he knew was how she moved with him on that floor like they'd been doing it for years and could do it for many more. Most of all, he knew how the impossible felt in his arms.

He sat on the porch until the night cooled down, which could take a long time in the spring, but not long enough on this night. He went inside and lay on his bed in the dark.

He was in trouble. He'd known it for days. But knowing hadn't changed anything. What changed things was a dance, a woman taking his hand and falling into sync with his steps. And when it was over, it was all he could do to let go.

CHAPTER TEN

Bobby made her bed, brushed her teeth, and went to the kitchen at 7:15 a.m., like it was any other morning.

But it was not any other morning. Her body knew the difference, even if her brain refused to cooperate. She had slept badly and woken early, and the first thing she'd been aware of was the weight of his hand on her waist, which was a memory, not a sensation, and she had no business confusing the two. She'd lain in the narrow bunk and stared at the ceiling and told herself, very firmly, that a dance was a dance. People danced. It was a Saturday night activity in most of the civilized world. The fact that her skin still held the warmth of his palm through the fabric of her shirt was a physiological event, not a romantic one, and she was going to take a shower and move on.

She took a shower. She did not entirely move on.

The kitchen was warm and busy when she came through the screen door. Ruby was at the stove, making scrambled eggs, and Denny was at the table with a glass of orange juice and a schoolbook open in front of him. Judd was at his usual spot with coffee. The radio was on low. Everything was exactly where it belonged, and Bobby said good morning, poured herself coffee, and slid into her chair. She was, in every measurable way, normal.

Bobby did not look toward the barn or ask where Wyatt was. She wondered, but she couldn't help her thoughts. She buttered a piece of toast and ate it, had a second cup of coffee, and talked to Ruby about possible items to include in the subscription box. If her voice was a fraction too bright and her posture a fraction too upright, nobody seemed to notice, except Bobby.

Wyatt came in when she was on her third cup. He hung his hat on the hook by the door and sat down at the head of the table.

"Morning," he said to the table in general.

"Morning," Bobby said to her coffee cup in particular.

Ruby looked at Bobby, whose eyes flickered away. Ruby put a plate in front of Wyatt. He said thank you and ate. Just another normal morning on the Cavanaugh Creek Ranch. Except Bobby felt his presence the way she felt the stove's warmth from across the room, constant and impossible to ignore.

Bobby looked at the window. Outside, a mockingbird was making a racket in the live oak, cycling through a repertoire of stolen songs with the confidence of a performer who had never been told to stop. Bobby watched the bird, drank her coffee, and decided that mockingbirds were fascinating.

THE SMOKER HAD BEEN GOING since before dawn.

Bobby smelled it when she stepped off the bunkhouse porch that morning and again when she crossed the yard after breakfast, and by midday the whole ranch carried it, a slow, sweet, rolling scent of oak smoke and rendered fat that hung in the warm air like the weather. It was different from the usual campfire smell that drifted through the property when Judd burned brush. This was deeper and richer, layered with something that Bobby's nose couldn't break into its parts, but its whole was nothing short of amazing. She kept catching it and turning toward it the way you turn toward a song that you love.

Judd was tending the smoker when she walked over to him in the early afternoon. He sat in his lawn chair beside the big offset drum with a Shiner in one hand and a spray bottle in the other. The smoker was working, thin blue smoke curling from the chimney stack at the far end, and the firebox door was cracked an inch. Judd's eyes moved between the thermometer gauge welded to the lid and something only he could see.

"How long has that been going?" Bobby asked.

"Started her at four."

"This morning?"

He looked at her as though the answer were self-evident.

She did the math. Ten hours and counting, with a few more to go. Judd had been sitting with this smoker, or close to it, since before the sun came up.

He'd fed the firebox through the cool morning hours, kept the temperature in whatever range he considered correct, sprayed the meat at intervals he'd worked out over three decades, and done it all with the patient, unhurried attention of a man whose relationship to time was not the same as other people's.

"Can I watch?" she asked.

"You've been watching."

"Can I watch closer?"

He looked at her the way he looked at everything, as though the question had a weight he needed to assess before he answered it. Then he tilted his head toward the empty folding chair beside him.

Bobby sat. She didn't reach for her camera. Her instincts told her this wasn't the moment.

Judd sprayed the inside of the lid with something from the bottle, apple cider vinegar from the smell, and closed it. He settled back in his chair and crossed one boot over the other.

"Brisket's not complicated," he said. "People make it complicated. It's salt, pepper, smoke, and time. That's all you need if you've got the right wood and the patience to leave it alone." He took a drink of his beer. "Problem is, most people don't have the patience to leave anything alone."

"Just salt and pepper?"

He looked at her with sparkling eyes. "And a few other things."

She sat with him for the better part of an hour. He didn't narrate. He opened the firebox twice to add a split of mesquite. Once he lifted the lid and sprayed the meat, Bobby saw it for the first time. Two full briskets lay side by side on the grate, dark as mahogany, the fat cap glistening. The heat that came off the open lid hit her face like a wall. Judd closed it, sat back down, and picked up his beer as though he'd done nothing more strenuous than check his mailbox.

When the light went golden and the shadows stretched long from the barn, Judd stood up and said, "Give me about two hours."

THEY HAD brisket for supper that evening.

Ruby had set the table the way she always did, but there was an empty space in the center. Judd finished slicing the meat at the counter, carried the board to the table, and set it down with the measured care of a man presenting evidence in court. The meat lay in even slices, with the bark almost black along the edge and the interior pink and glistening.

Bobby looked at the brisket and then looked at Judd. He was watching her and, for once, his face wasn't guarded. There was an expectancy in it, an alertness she hadn't seen from him before, as though his brisket was about to be judged and the verdict was not entirely within his control.

She picked up a slice with her fingers. The meat was so juicy and tender it nearly came apart in her hand.

She took a bite.

The first thing she tasted was smoke, deep and round, not sharp or acrid. Then came salt, coarse black pepper, and beneath those, the beef itself—rich and clean, with a sweetness in the fat that dissolved on her tongue. A warmth built slowly at the back of her mouth. She chewed, swallowed, and sat very still.

Judd watched.

Bobby looked at him. She opened her mouth and the intended compliment came out as a small involuntary noise in the back of her throat that was worth more than any word she could have chosen.

Judd nodded once.

Bobby took another bite. She closed her eyes this time, because there was too much going on at the table, with the chatter, the faces, and Denny reaching for the cornbread. She needed a moment. Whatever those seven spices were, they had woven into the smoke and the salt, and she couldn't separate them, except for the pepper.

She opened her eyes. Ruby was smiling. Denny had a piece in each hand. Wyatt was eating with the quiet focus of a man who'd been eating Judd's brisket his whole life and understood what it was without needing to be told.

"Judd!" Bobby stared wide-eyed. "How long did it take you to get this right?"

He considered the question. "I'll let you know when I do."

After supper, Bobby was carrying dishes to the sink when Judd appeared in the kitchen doorway. He stood there until she noticed him. His hands were in his pockets and his hat was on, which meant he was about to go somewhere, or at least pretend to be on his way somewhere so this conversation would be short.

"I tell you what. I'll let you photograph the process," he said. "Next time I fire her up."

Bobby set the dishes in the sink. "The whole thing?"

"Not the rub recipe, but you can watch the rest, if you want."

She did want. She wanted it very much. She also understood what was being offered. Judd's smoker, Judd's method, and the thirty years of trial and correction that had produced what she'd tasted at that table. These were not things he shared. He'd told her seven spices on the first day and hadn't said another word since. This wasn't an invitation to a cooking demonstration. It was the closest thing to trust that Judd had to give.

"I'd be honored," she said, and meant it.

He nodded and walked out into the dark, and she stood at the sink with her hands in the warm water and thought about the flavor of brisket and the man who'd spent thirty years refining something most people would have declared beyond perfect decades ago.

ON MONDAY MORNING, an Indian paintbrush had pushed through a crack in the bunkhouse step.

The bluebonnets had been going strong for a couple of weeks now, rolling through the pastures in waves of blue that deepened every morning. But lately the Indian paintbrushes had started coming in alongside them, streaks of fiery red-orange threading through the blue, and from a distance the fields looked like something Bobby would have dismissed as over-saturated if she'd seen it in someone else's photograph.

She almost stepped on this one. She had her camera bag over one shoulder and her coffee in her free hand, and she was halfway down the steps when that splotch of red caught her eye and she stopped. A single stem, no taller than her hand, had found a gap in the limestone where the step met the foundation. The crack was barely wide enough to fit a pencil. The paintbrush had pushed through it anyway, its soft red bristles reaching up past the stone.

She set her coffee on the porch railing and crouched. The stem was bent slightly where it had fought its way through, and the leaves were dusty from the foot traffic that had passed within inches of it for however long it had been growing there. It shouldn't have survived. The crack was too narrow, the stone too heavy, the path too busy. But here it was, stubborn, crimson, and blooming where no one would expect it.

Bobby looked at it for a long time, then she took one close-up photograph of the red against the gray, and moved on.

KAY CALLED HER THAT AFTERNOON.

Bobby was on the bunkhouse porch with her laptop, organizing the food photographs she'd taken over the past week: Ruby's kolaches in morning light, the baked beans with Judd's secret ingredient, diced pears, in a cast-iron crock, and a loaf of jalapeño cornbread cooling on a rack. Good, clean product shots with the ranch in the background. She answered on the third ring.

"The proofs are in," Kay said. "Bobby, they're stunning."

"Yeah?"

"The creek shot. The barn at sunrise. That portrait of the old man by the smoker, the one where the light's coming through the smoke and he looks like he's been carved out of mesquite." Kay's voice had the energy it got when she was excited about work—clipped, bright, and hard to slow down. "These are some of the best things you've ever shot."

Bobby smiled and looked across the yard. Judd was walking toward the equipment shed with a fence post over one shoulder and the unhurried gait of a man who would get there when he got there.

"I'm glad," Bobby said. "I'm really glad."

"The magazine's thrilled. They're talking about the August cover, which, you know, never happens with a ranch piece. You've got something special here."

Bobby waited because she knew Kay. The energy in Kay's voice hadn't peaked yet. There was a gear shift coming.

"Listen," Kay said. "I've been sitting with these proofs for a few days, and I've been thinking about something."

There it was.

"The financial angle," Kay said. "Not for this piece. The assignment is done. It's beautiful, and it stands on its own. But there's a bigger story here. Heritage ranchers and family operations are going under because the system is designed to squeeze them out. The import quotas, the meatpacker consolidation, all of it. Your ranch isn't the only one facing this. There are hundreds of them across Texas, and most of them won't survive the next decade."

Bobby's hand tightened on the phone. She didn't speak.

"It's a powerful issue, like many faced by the flyover states, which the rest of us tend to forget," Kay said. "I'm talking about an advocacy piece. The kind that puts a human face on the numbers. One ranch, one family, one version of a story that's happening everywhere." She paused. "Cavanaugh Creek would be the centerpiece. The Cavanaughs' story is compelling. It's real. And your access, your photographs, they'd make it undeniable."

Bobby looked at the screen door of the main house, where Ruby had hung a dish towel to dry on the railing. Through the kitchen window, she could see the edge of the table where they all sat every evening.

"Kay," she said.

"I know. I know it's a lot."

"What made you think…? I mean, I never said that the ranch was in trouble."

It's a ranch. It's in trouble. An article on a financial website caught my eye because we're doing this story. So I did some more research. This could be so much more than a beautiful piece of Americana. It's a portrait of an American era.

She didn't have to say any more. Bobby knew what she meant.

"And I'm not asking you to decide right now. Just think about it. The piece could do real good, Bobby. It could change the conversation."

"It could also put this family's finances in a spotlight they didn't ask for."

"That's why I'm asking you instead of going around you. Because you know these people. You'd know how to tell the story right."

Bobby searched for words.

"You could help them."

Bobby pressed her lips together. Kay wasn't wrong. The story was real, and the numbers were devastating, and she'd sat at that kitchen table and heard enough from Ruby, Judd—and even Wyatt, in his spare, careful way—to understand what was happening to ranches like this one. The drought, the import quotas, the four meatpacking corporations that controlled eighty-five percent of the processing and paid ranchers less than thirty cents of every retail dollar. It wasn't a secret. It was an industry-wide crisis that most Americans never thought about when they bought a steak at the grocery store.

But telling that story meant telling Wyatt's story. The back taxes, the herd being cut in half, and the crew reduced to family members and occasional help from their neighbors. Wyatt Cavanaugh was a man who would rather lose his ranch than ask for help, and this piece would be the loudest form of asking for help she could imagine.

"Let me think about it," Bobby said.

"Take your time. No deadline. I just wanted to plant the seed."

They talked about logistics for another minute—the magazine layout schedule, the publication timeline, and whether they'd need a reshoot of any interiors. Bobby answered on autopilot. When Kay hung up, Bobby sat on the porch with her phone in her lap and looked at the ranch in the late afternoon light.

The yard was quiet. The cattle had moved to the far pasture, past the line of mesquite trees that marked the property's western fence. A scissortail flycatcher sat on the fence wire nearest the barn, its long, forked tail twitching. From somewhere behind the house, she could hear the faint clang of Wyatt working on something metal, a gate hinge or a trailer coupling, with the steady rhythm of a man who would keep fixing things until there was nothing left to fix.

She thought about the word "centerpiece," and imagined Wyatt's face if he ever saw his ranch's financial troubles laid bare in a national magazine.

She closed her laptop and went inside to eat supper with the family. She laughed at something Denny said, helped Ruby clear the table, said good night, and walked back to the bunkhouse under starlight.

In the dark, on her bunk, she lay listening to the ranch as it settled down to sleep. The now familiar sounds of the creek, the cattle, the breeze in the cedar and the live oak felt as much a part of this ranch as the people in it, as if each piece of land and everything on it held a memory of the three generations who'd worked, lived, and loved here on a ranch that might not survive a fourth.

She stared at the ceiling. Kay's offer was generous, and the story was important. She was right about that. But the family on the other side of that yard had let her into their home, lives, and kitchen. She could still taste Judd's brisket on her tongue, and she could still feel the weight of Wyatt's hand on her waist.

She did not sleep well.

CHAPTER ELEVEN

THE NUMBERS DIDN'T WORK.

Wyatt sat at his father's desk with his phone in his hand and a spreadsheet on his laptop. Beside him lay a yellow legal pad full of figures that he'd written, crossed out, rewritten, and crossed out again. The scarred oak desk had been in the same corner of the office since his grandfather ordered it from a catalog in 1962. The leather blotter was cracked down the middle. A jar of pens, most of which didn't write anymore, sat at the back edge beside a framed photograph of Pop and his mother at a cattle auction in 1987. Pop was grinning. His mother was squinting into the sun and holding a funnel cake.

Layton, the banker, was a courteous man with the uncanny ability to say no without ever using the actual word. Restructuring the note on the south herd was not, at this time, an option the bank could extend. The interest rate had already been adjusted. The payment schedule remained as agreed. If Mr.

Cavanaugh wished to explore alternative avenues, the bank would be happy to discuss options at his convenience.

Alternative avenues. Wyatt knew what that meant. It meant selling something. The south herd, the back pasture, the equipment shed, and the tractor inside it. It meant carving off a piece of the ranch and handing it over so the rest could survive another year, maybe two, until the next drought, the next quota adjustment, or the next quarterly report from one of the four corporations that controlled the price of every steer he raised.

He set the phone on the desk and looked at the legal pad. He'd worked the figures three ways. The subscription box orders could mean real money, eventually. But not enough for now. Not yet. Two hundred orders at forty-two dollars a box came to just over eight thousand a month before costs. And the costs were higher than Ruby wanted to admit, because Ruby had never shipped anything in her life and didn't know what dry ice and USDA labeling ran. If the magazine spread generated those kinds of numbers and the orders kept climbing, it might cover the note payment by September. That was five months of holding on.

He'd been holding on for years, and it was wearing him down.

The calculator didn't care. He closed the app and put the phone in his pocket and sat there in the chair that Pop had sat in when the ranch ran twice as many head and employed a full crew, when the biggest worry was whether the spring rains would come on time.

He stood up and went outside.

THE MORNING WAS warm and bright. A south wind had come up overnight and brought with it the dry, sage-green smell of the open country beyond the ranch's southern fence. The barn swallows were chattering in the eaves. Bobby's rental car was parked by the bunkhouse. She was around, but he didn't want to see her right now. He didn't want to see anyone right now. He just wanted to ride fence and think.

He was saddling Shadow when Ruby came around the corner of the barn with her apron on and her sleeves pushed up past the elbows. She looked as though something was on her mind. "Layton called back?"

"I called him."

She folded her arms and waited.

"It wasn't good news."

Ruby leaned against the stall door. She didn't need to ask more. "What are you thinking?"

"I'm thinking I need to ride the east fence line. Some posts looked loose when I was out last week."

"Wyatt."

"The numbers don't work, Ruby. Not this month. Maybe not next month. Your box idea is going to help, but not soon enough."

She was quiet. He tightened the cinch and ran his

hand along Shadow's neck. The horse's ears twitched forward.

"I'll figure it out," he said. "I always do."

"I know you do," she said gently.

He pulled the bridle off the hook and turned back to Shadow. Ruby watched him for a minute. Then she said, "Take Bobby with you."

He stopped. "No."

"She hasn't seen the east side of the property, and she's been wanting to ride again since the valley."

"I don't need company."

"I didn't say that you did. I said take Bobby." Ruby crossed her arms. "She's been sitting on the bunkhouse porch all morning with her laptop. She looks restless. And you look like a man who's about to go ride for four hours and stew in his own head, which is what you do every time Layton calls. Brooding alone never helps."

"Ruby."

"I'll go tell her."

She left before he could argue. He stood in the barn with the bridle in his hands, the horse waiting, and the south wind pushing through the open doors. He could have gone after her. He could have said no again and meant it. Instead, he finished tacking up and led Shadow to the water trough and stood there in the sun.

The screen door opened and shut. Bobby crossed the yard with her camera bag on her shoulder and a look on her face that was trying to be casual. She'd changed into a flannel shirt over a T-shirt, and her hair was in that low knot she wore when she was working. She stopped a few feet from the water trough.

"Ruby said you might have room for a passenger."

"Ruby says a lot of things."

Bobby stood there. He could feel her deciding whether to push it or let him be.

"It looks like my timing is bad. It's just that Ruby said…"

The timing was terrible. He'd just gotten off the phone with a man who all but told him the ranch was running out of runway, and the last thing he needed was an afternoon alone with a woman he'd spent every waking hour since Saturday night failing to put out of his mind. But Bobby was standing in the sun with her camera bag and her ropers, and she wasn't pushing, and the alternative was riding out alone with the legal pad and Layton's voice in his head.

Before she could finish, he said, "Saddle's in the tack room. Same one as last time. Dolly's in the second stall."

She went to get the saddle. He noticed she didn't need to ask which one.

THEY RODE east along the fence line that followed the creek's upper branch, past the third gate and the old cedar break where the trail narrowed to single file. The country opened up beyond the break into rolling grassland that stretched to the eastern hills, and Wyatt let Shadow find his own pace. Dolly fell into step beside him, and Bobby rode the way she'd ridden in the valley, quiet, easy in the saddle, and her eyes on the land.

He didn't talk. She didn't seem to need him to.

They checked four posts along the upper run. Two were solid. Two were leaning where the clay had softened in the last rain. He dismounted and tamped them with the flat of his boot and then made a mental note to come back with the post driver. Bobby stayed mounted and watched. Once she lifted the camera and took a shot of him working. He heard the shutter, but didn't look up.

It was Bobby who spoke first, half a mile past the second gate, where the trail ran along a ridge, and the whole east pasture lay below them.

"Can I ask you something? Not about the ranch. About ranching."

He looked at her. "Go ahead."

"The import quotas. The ones on beef from South America. How bad is it?"

He rode for a few strides before answering. "Bad enough. Argentina's been flooding the market since the last quota increase. We can't compete on price. Their labor costs are a fraction of ours, and the packers buy on volume."

"The packers being the four big companies."

"They set the price, and the price hasn't kept up with costs in a decade." He said it evenly, the way he'd say it to anyone who asked. These were facts. Public record. Nothing personal about them.

Bobby said, "So as a small, grass-fed operation, you're competing against industrial beef on a playing field that isn't level."

"That's about the size of it."

"And the drought?"

"Three years running. Not as bad as 2011, but bad enough to thin the herd. We sold off one hundred fifty head in two seasons because the pasture wouldn't carry them."

She looked at him attentively. "What happens to ranches that can't hold on?"

"They sell." He paused. "Sometimes in pieces. Sometimes the whole thing. A developer buys it, or an investment group, or some outfit that wants to run longhorns as a tax shelter and never touches the land."

"And the families?"

"They leave."

She was quiet after that. He could feel her processing it, turning the information over the way she'd examine a photo, looking at it from different angles. He'd answered her questions honestly. It was all common knowledge. Ranchers all over the Hill Country were facing the same thing. It was in all the farm journals and the county extension bulletins. Even the newspapers ran an occasional piece in the back pages where nobody looked.

But the conversation had drifted close to the bone. She was talking about the industry, and he was hearing his own ranch in every sentence. The bank call was still sitting in his chest like a stone, and the more she asked, the harder it was to answer in generalities when his own specifics were right there closing in on him. Back taxes. The south herd note. Layton's measured voice.

He'd rather lose the whole ranch than look like a man who couldn't handle it.

"Most operations find a way," he said, and he could hear the door closing in his own voice.

Bobby must have heard it too. She nodded and looked away, down the slope to where the cattle grazed in the lower pasture, and she didn't ask anything else.

They rode in uncomfortable silence. He'd pulled back, and he sensed that she knew it and chose not to follow up with more questions. The horses' hooves on the hard ground and the creak of saddle leather and the wind in the grass were the only sounds, and Wyatt was grateful for every one of them.

He was mid-thought, something about the feed order, when the wind stopped.

Sounds that were always just there suddenly were not. The south wind that had been steady since morning just quit. The grass stopped moving. The leaves on the live oaks hung still, and the air felt thick and close.

He looked up.

The western sky had changed. Where it had been hard blue all morning, a band of gray-green was building above the hills, dark and moving fast. The undersides of the clouds were the color of a bruise, and the light had shifted.

Wyatt reined Shadow to a stop. Bobby stopped beside him.

"What's wrong?" she said.

He didn't answer right away. He was reading the sky the way his father had taught him, and his grandfather before that—the way the air felt thick with moisture, the pressure of it against his face, and the smell of it. The temperature had dropped three or four degrees in the last couple of minutes, and the swallows were gone.

Bobby followed his gaze to the west. The cloud line was building fast now, the tops boiling upward in a vertical lift, and below that, a shelf of darker cloud was pushing ahead of the front like a plow blade.

"We need to go," he said. "Now."

She looked at him. Whatever she saw in his face was enough. She didn't ask questions.

He turned Shadow west, toward the old line shack on the far side of the creek crossing. The house was forty minutes at a walk and twenty at a lope, and they didn't have twenty minutes. The line shack was ten, maybe less if they pushed.

He kicked Shadow into a fast trot and heard Dolly match the pace behind him. He didn't look back. He didn't need to. Bobby was a good enough rider, Dolly knew the way, and what was coming behind them wasn't going to wait for anyone.

The first gust hit them at the creek crossing, a wall of warm air that smelled like dust and ozone. The trees along the creek bent hard to the east, and leaves and small branches tore free and spun past them. He glanced back and saw Bobby's flannel whip against her arms. Dolly pinned her ears and broke into a canter.

He spotted the line shack through the trees. It was a small limestone building with a tin roof, one room, built by his grandfather in 1956 and used by every generation since as shelter when the sky turned and you were too far from the house to make it home.

The light went green. He'd seen that light twice in his life, and both times the storm that followed had taken down fences, trees, and anything else that wasn't built to last. The air pressure dropped so fast his ears popped.

"Stay with me," he said over his shoulder, and he pushed Shadow the last hundred yards to the shack.

CHAPTER TWELVE

THE LINE SHACK was smaller than she'd imagined.

One room. A narrow cot against the back wall, a cast-iron woodstove in the corner with a flue pipe running up through the ceiling, and a kerosene lantern on a shelf beside a tin of matches. The floor was packed limestone, smooth from decades of boot traffic, and the walls were the same rough-cut stone as the main house but thinner, laid without mortar in places, so hairline gaps of daylight showed between the blocks. A single window, no bigger than a breadbox, sat high on the east wall. The glass was old, wavy, and thick with dust.

Wyatt had the door open before she'd finished looking around. He was moving fast now, faster than she'd ever seen him move, and she understood that whatever he'd seen in the sky on the ride over had not gotten better.

"Inside," he said.

She went. He didn't follow. Through the doorway,

she watched him untie Shadow from the iron ring, pull Dolly's reins free, and slap both horses hard on the flank. They bolted. Shadow went south toward the creek bottom, Dolly followed, and within seconds they were gone, running flat and fast with their ears back and their tails streaming.

She stared at the empty space where the horses had been.

Wyatt came through the door, pulled it shut, and dropped the wooden bar into the brackets. He crossed to the window and looked out, but didn't say anything. His jaw was set, and his breathing was controlled.

"Wyatt."

"Don't talk for a second."

She didn't talk. She stood in the middle of the room and watched him watch the sky, and the first thing she noticed was the sound. Or the absence of it. The wind had stopped. The birds had stopped. The insects had stopped. The world outside the line shack had gone eerily silent, instinctively making the hair on her arms stand up.

Then the light changed.

It happened all at once. The daylight coming through the gaps in the stone shifted from gray to green, a sick yellow-green she had never seen before, and the air pressure dropped so fast that her ears popped.

"Get down," Wyatt said. "Against that wall. Sit on the floor and put your back against the stone."

She did it. She slid down the wall beside the woodstove and pulled her knees to her chest. He was still at the window.

"What is it?" she said, though she already knew it wasn't good. She'd seen the Weather Channel.

"Tornado." He said it the way he said everything, level and factual, except his knuckles were white on the window frame. "Southwest. Maybe two miles out."

"Two miles?"

"Could be less." He turned from the window and looked at her. "This shack has stood since 1956. It's not going anywhere now."

She believed him because she trusted him, and because she had no other choice.

He sat down beside her against the wall. Close. His shoulder against hers, his leg pressed against her leg. He was warm, solid, and smelled like leather, horses, and sweat. She realized her hands were shaking, but she couldn't make them stop.

Outside, the silence broke.

It started as a low hum, a vibration she felt in the floor before she heard it in the air. Then it grew. The hum became a rumble, and the rumble became a roar, a deep, sustained, mechanical sound that did not belong in the natural world. She'd heard people describe it as a freight train. They were wrong. It was deeper than that, more primal, a sound that came up through the earth, through the stone walls, and into her bones. The tin roof began to rattle. The gaps between the stones let in thin streams of dust, and the kerosene lantern slid three inches across the shelf without anyone touching it.

Wyatt put his arm around her. He pulled her against his chest and held the back of her head with his other hand and pressed her face into his shoulder. She could feel his heart through his shirt, beating hard and steady, and she held on to the front of his collar with both fists and closed her eyes.

The roar built. The walls shook. Something struck the outside of the shack, a hard crack against the stone that could have been a branch or a fence post or anything the wind had picked up and thrown. The tin roof screamed. She thought: This is how it ends—in Texas, in a building the size of her apartment, and in the arms of a man she'd known for eleven days.

Then the sound shifted.

The roar pulled east, and the vibration in the floor lessened by a degree and then another degree, and then it was fading, not gone but moving away, tracking across the pasture toward the creek and the hills beyond. The tin roof settled. The dust stopped streaming through the gaps. The lantern was still on the shelf.

Wyatt didn't let go.

She didn't move. She stayed against his chest with her face in his shoulder and her fists in his collar while the tornado left. The sound dimmed from a roar to a rumble to a low, distant hum, and then it was gone, and the rain took its place. Hard rain, a curtain of water that hit the tin roof and filled the room with a sustained drumming that was, after what they'd just heard, almost gentle.

"It turned," he said. His voice was rough. His hand was still on the back of her head. "Went east."

She nodded against his shoulder. She was trembling. The delayed reaction moved through her in waves she couldn't stop. She'd never been that close to dying before. She'd never heard a sound like that or known that fear could be a physical thing that lived in your chest and your stomach.

His arm tightened around her. His chin rested on top of her head. He held her the way he held everything he was trying to protect: completely and without reservation, shielding her with both arms and his whole body between her and whatever was outside.

The rain had settled into a steady, heavy drumming on the tin roof, the kind of rain that could go all night. Through the high window, the sky was dark. The air inside the shack was thick, close, and smelled like dust, sweat, and rain.

"It's okay," he whispered as he kissed her forehead. "It's okay."

She lifted her head. He was staring at the far wall, and the gray light from the window caught the hard line of his jaw and the tension in it. Then he turned, and his eyes locked onto hers.

He was right there. His face inches from hers, his eyes dark in the gray half-light, and on his face she saw something she'd never seen before. Gone was the reserve, the set jaw, and the measured calm he wore like armor. It may have been the aftermath of fear. She felt it too. They'd been so close to losing their lives and each other. And in that moment, all the rules and the walls she'd built up didn't matter. They were here now, together. It was their second chance. And then, as the fear drained from their bodies, something else replaced it—something raw took its place, and she couldn't get close enough to this man who meant everything to her.

She didn't think about what happened next. Nothing mattered except putting her mouth on his. She took hold of his face, and she kissed him.

He went still for a second. His whole body stiffened with surprise and restraint, and every reason this was a bad idea. She felt him fight it, and she felt the exact moment when every rational objection he'd been carrying for eleven days lost the fight against what he desperately wanted.

He kissed her back until she doubted she'd ever really been kissed before this.

His hand came up to her jaw, and his mouth opened against hers. Her head swam as he kissed her the way he did everything—with thorough, unbridled intent, with his whole body behind it. His hand slid from her jaw into her hair, and she pulled him closer by the front of his shirt, and the kiss deepened until not even a tornado could have torn them apart.

He pulled back, breathing ragged, hand still in her hair, and he said, "Bobby." That was all. But she heard it as a question.

"Yes," she said.

He looked at her in the gray light, and she watched him decide. The last bit of resistance went out of his face, and he kissed her again. Harder. His hands found her waist and pulled her into his lap, and she went, her knees on either side of his hips, her back against his hands. The rain pounded the tin roof loudly enough to drown out everything except the sound of his breathing and hers.

She pulled his shirt free and put her hands on his skin. He was so warm. His mouth was on her neck, his hands were in her hair, and outside the rain went on and on. Inside the line shack, there were no rules left. Just the two of them, the dark, and the rain on the tin.

CHAPTER THIRTEEN

THE RAIN HAD STOPPED.

Bobby knew it before she opened her eyes. The tin roof had gone quiet. For hours, it had been the only sound, steady and heavy, drumming out the world beyond these four stone walls. Now the silence was enormous. Air came through the gaps in the mortar, carrying the sweetness of wildflowers, grasses, and damp earth.

Together, they lay on the cot, Bobby on her side, Wyatt behind her with the length of his body along hers, and his arm draped over her waist. When his breathing changed, she knew he was awake, but they both lay still, not wanting the moment to end.

Gray light came through the high window. It wasn't quite dawn. She would have this moment to feel the weight of his arm and his warmth at her back. This was all of him she would have.

He withdrew his arm, kissed the back of her neck, and said, "We have to go."

She knew, but she couldn't bring herself to say it.

Wyatt got up first. She shut her eyes and willed time to stop, but it didn't. She had no choice but to follow suit. In silence, they found their discarded clothing and dressed.

Wyatt opened the door and stood with his hands braced on the frame, looking out at his land. She'd watched him like this a dozen times before—the set of his shoulders, the stillness in his spine. Except now she'd had her hands on those shoulders. She knew what the skin felt like beneath the shirt, and the memory would not release her.

When he turned to face her, their eyes met and held. She saw everything she felt reflected at her. Shadow appeared at the door, and Wyatt went to him. Bobby watched them, tears rising.

Wyatt turned and said, "Dolly's not with him. We'll have to go find her." With no further explanation, he mounted Shadow, then held out his hand. Bobby took it and sat behind him.

The Hill Country after the storm defied preparation. The sky was enormous and pale, deep blue overhead, fading to peach along the eastern hills. The land was washed clean. Steam rose where the early sun touched the ground, and the air smelled like rain. The beauty of it deepened the ache.

They rode to the creek. Wyatt whistled, but the sound returned empty. After two more calls, an answering nicker came from further along. Dolly appeared through the cedars and walked through wet brush with her ears forward and her coat dark with moisture.

Wyatt took Bobby's hand and steadied her as she swung out of the saddle, then he got down and tended to Dolly. When he'd straightened the saddle and tightened the cinch, he looked at her and said, "Ready?"

Everything they would not say passed between them. She saw it in his raw, unwary expression, the one she'd first seen in the kerosene lantern light when he'd kissed her. He loved her. She could see it as clearly as the color of his eyes, and it terrified her because she loved him back.

He looked away first and checked Dolly's cinch again.

She crossed the wet ground and put her hand on his arm. He went still. His hand covered hers. His thumb moved once across her knuckles. The next second, they were in each other's arms while the steam rose, the horses waited, and the Hill Country stretched out, indifferent to them.

Bobby stepped back, and he let her go.

They rode in silence: four miles of wet pasture, cedar breaks, limestone slick from rain. Single file, Wyatt leading on Shadow. She watched his back, his broad shoulders, the way he sat a horse, and the line of his hat against the sky.

When they came over the last ridge, the ranch spread out below them with the limestone house, the barn, and the bunkhouse against a washed-out morning sky. Ruby rushed through the kitchen door and stood in the yard wiping her tears. "Do you know how worried I've been?"

Wyatt was off Shadow in one motion. He had his arms around his sister before Bobby had gotten her feet out of the stirrups. "We're okay," he said. "We sheltered in the line shack. We're fine."

When Ruby pulled back and let go, she said, "The Dawsons lost two sections of fence and a hay barn. Earl called me at four in the morning, looking for you. I didn't know what to tell him because I didn't know if you—"

"We're here."

Ruby looked at Bobby beside Dolly, then wrapped her arms around her. Bobby hugged her back and felt Ruby shaking. "I'm okay," Bobby said. Ruby squeezed tighter, then let go. She wiped her face and looked at both of them, at first with relief, but then with a sharp awareness of the silence between them. She kept it to herself. "Coffee's on," she said.

Judd was standing at the corner of the barn with a feed bucket in one hand. He took one look at Bobby, another at Wyatt, then set the bucket down and walked over to them. He took both horses' reins and, without a word, led them toward the barn without looking back.

Bobby went to the bunkhouse to shower. She stood under the water for a long time. When she dressed and looked in the mirror over the sink, she didn't recognize herself: a woman in love with a man rooted to two thousand acres of Texas. Nothing would change that. Leaving was going to cost her.

In the kitchen, Ruby had coffee, eggs, and biscuits laid out. Despite the sleepless night, she moved with her usual determined energy.

"So, you were stuck out in the storm," Ruby said as she reached for the butter.

"The line shack."

Ruby set the butter on the table and sat across from her. She looked at Bobby just long enough to show the questions she was choosing not to ask. Ruby was not a fool. She'd spent the night fearing the worst, and now the two of them wouldn't meet each other's eyes. She knew.

She couldn't pretend not to care for Wyatt, nor could she lie to Ruby. "I need to run into Kerrville. Camera supplies and photos to cull." The excuses tumbled out.

Bobby rinsed her mug and put it in the dishwasher. The screen door opened. Wyatt came in, showered, his hair still damp. He stood in the kitchen looking at her. Ruby turned away from both of them.

The look in his eyes broke Bobby. "Excuse me." She slipped past him.

Wyatt followed. "Can we talk?"

"If talking could change anything, I would." Her voice was quieter than she meant it to be.

His face didn't move. She turned and went back to the bunkhouse for her bag and keys.

She made it to the end of the ranch road before her hands started shaking. She drove until the ranch was out of sight, then pulled over.

After she'd had a good cry, she drove into Kerrville and parked in front of Hank's camera shop. She handed Hank a thumb drive and asked for an 11 x 14 print in a simple wood frame with a cream-colored mat. She asked if he could do a rush job on it.

Hank said, "Give me two hours."

At the diner, coffee and her laptop. She was

supposed to cull the archive. Instead, she scrolled through photos she hadn't been hired to take. All of Wyatt.

Wyatt at the fence line in the late light, one boot on the rail. Wyatt in the barn doorway, dust motes suspended around him. Wyatt on horseback at the ridge, silhouetted against the sky. Wyatt at the supper table, turning, his face unguarded in a way she'd only seen a few times.

She closed the laptop, finished her coffee, and left.

On Wednesday, she threw herself into work in Ruby's kitchen. Ruby cooked while Bobby reviewed photographs, logo design, and the marketing plan. By afternoon, they were deep in it, laptops open at the cleared kitchen table, their to-do list taking shape: Judd's brisket rub in Kraft paper with custom stickers and kolaches in cellophane wrappers, both frozen; Judd's baked beans in pint-sized Mason jars; jalapeño cornbread mix in muslin with a recipe card tied on with string; a small pecan pie boxed with Denny's monthly photo. All of it shipped overnight.

"People aren't just buying beef," Bobby said, sketching on the back of Ruby's legal pad. "They're buying something made the old-fashioned way. Farm-sourced. A piece of heritage in a delicious package. Every item has someone's name: Wyatt's beef, Judd's rub, Ruby's kolaches, Denny's photos. You're not providing a product; you're giving them a seat at your table."

Ruby watched her. "It's not just our family. It's you. Your photos and designs. Please help with the launch."

Bobby kept her eyes on the sketch. "Of course." She added, "I'll be back home, but I can do my part remotely."

Ruby said nothing. The silence held what Bobby had just said, how it sounded, how far it was from what she wanted.

"Wednesday," Ruby said as she stood. "Pecan pie. You promised."

After cleanup, Bobby sat at the kitchen table with her sketchpad and coffee, working on packaging: box dimensions, label placement, photo position, tissue folds. She drew the Cavanaugh Creek mark in pencil, then erased and redrew it. She was having more fun than in years. The kitchen was warm, smelling of pecans and pastry. Outside, she could hear Judd puttering around. Through the window, the Hill Country sky was painting its sunset in gold and silver, too beautiful for a real place.

She realized she hadn't thought about the line shack in twenty minutes. She erased the mark one more time and drew it again.

CHAPTER FOURTEEN

Bobby was laughing at something Ruby said.

Wyatt stood in the hallway outside the kitchen and listened to her full-throated laugh, the kind that came out without thinking. He'd heard it once at the rodeo, once at the bar when Ruby was teaching her to line dance, and now here, in his family's kitchen, at seven o'clock on a Wednesday evening.

She was at the table with her laptop and legal pad beside her, drawing something with a pencil while Ruby stood at the counter wrapping leftovers. The overhead light caught the side of Bobby's face and lit up the line of her jaw, and she was leaning forward over the paper the way she leaned into her camera, with an intensity that made everything else disappear. Ruby said something else he couldn't hear, and Bobby laughed again, shook her head, and went back to her drawing.

When had she become part of the household? She fit. That was the problem. She fit without effort or company manners. She wasn't a guest anymore. She fit the way light fits when it shines through the window and fills every space with its warmth. She moved through Ruby's kitchen as though she'd grown up in it, and when she looked up at Ruby her face was open and entirely at home. And she fit in the worst way, because when she left, she would take her warmth with her and leave behind a cold space that would never be filled.

He must have moved or made a sound, because Ruby looked up and saw him in the doorway. Their eyes met. Ruby's expression was the one she'd been wearing since she was eleven years old, the one that meant she knew exactly what he was thinking. Worse, she knew, and she felt sorry for him. It was all in a gaze that lasted two seconds before she turned back to the counter and said nothing.

He walked away.

The house porch faced south, and the chairs on it were old wooden rockers that their father had bought at a farm auction in Hunt. They'd been sitting in the same spots for decades. Wyatt took the one on the left, put his boots up on the rail, and looked out at the dark. The Hill Country night was clear after the storm, and the sky was full of stars. The cattle were settling in for the night in the south pasture, and the creek, higher than it had been in months, made a new rushing sound. The rain had been good for the land. The land didn't care what else the storm had done.

He'd brought two Shiner Bocks from the refrigerator and set the second one on the rail for Judd. It took about ten minutes before he heard the boots on the porch steps. Judd joined him, sitting down in the chair the way he did everything: without ceremony. He just picked up the beer, twisted the cap off, and took a long drink.

They sat in silence. The night sounds filled in around them. Somewhere east of the creek, an owl worked the field edge, and the wind moved through the live oaks with the rustling whisper they make when the leaves are still wet.

"Earl called," Judd said.

"I know."

"He's going to need help with that fence."

"I'll ride over tomorrow."

More silence. Judd drank. Wyatt drank. There was no need for words when the beer was cold and the stars were where they were supposed to be.

Except Judd wasn't done.

"Bobby's really taken to ranch life," Judd said. His voice was the same flat, unhurried tone he used for everything, whether he was talking about the weather or the cattle or the single most important observation he'd made in the past two weeks. "She fits in pretty good around here."

Wyatt didn't answer. He turned the bottle in his hands, looked at the label, and didn't look at Judd.

Judd let the silence sit for a while. Then he finished his beer, set the empty one on the rail, and stood up. "Night," he said, and walked off the porch.

Wyatt sat watching the stars wheel overhead while the creek ran and the cattle made their low, distant sounds. He tried to keep his mind on the ranch because that was the thing he could think about without it tearing him open.

The numbers were bad. He'd known that for a while, but the letter from the bank last week had made them specific in a way that he couldn't ignore. The back pasture was the obvious piece to sell: a hundred twenty acres with a seasonal creek that dried up in August. It wasn't especially productive land, but not everyone saw it as farmland.

A developer from San Antonio had made an offer through Earl's real estate contact six months ago, and Wyatt shot back an immediate no. Cavanaughs did not sell their land. Cavanaughs also did not lose their ranch to the bank. They hadn't yet, anyway. But if feeder prices didn't recover by fall, the note on the south herd was going to come due with nothing behind it.

He could hear his father's voice, clear as the creek water. Hold on to the land because it's all that you've got. It's your legacy. His father had held onto the land until the day he died. Not only had he held onto the land passed down by his father, but he'd added to it with the back pasture acreage. But this ranch that his father had left him was a legacy of great pride and a greater burden. When his grandfather and father said to hold on to the land, they hadn't faced competition from imported beef, rising production costs, and price volatility.

But he'd managed to put off a call to his banker for one more day, so he finished his beer, set the empty beside Judd's, and sat there in the dark.

Bobby and Ruby came out through the kitchen

door about a half hour later. Ruby's dish towel was slung over her shoulder, and Bobby had a legal pad under her arm. They said their goodbyes for the night, and then Bobby saw him on the porch and went still for half a second. It was only a hitch in her step, just a fractional pause that anyone else would have missed.

She kept walking and said, "Good night, Wyatt," in a voice that was steady and warm.

"Night," he said.

Wyatt watched her walk to the bunkhouse until it was just him and the porch and the stars.

Inside the kitchen, Ruby had left the stove light on, the way she always did, and it cast a soft amber glow across the room.

Bobby had left her laptop on the table. It was open.

He'd meant to leave it alone, but on his way to get a glass of water, he walked by and glanced over. The screensaver was a slideshow of photos she'd taken.

The first one he saw was of him.

He was on horseback on the ridge, silhouetted against the sky. She'd shot it from below, so the horse, the land, and the sky took up the whole frame, and he was just a dark shape against the light on a Hill Country afternoon in late March.

The next slide was another photo of him. This one was a proof sheet, with dozens of thumbnails almost too small to make out. He leaned closer.

Every photo was of him.

They weren't the magazine shots he'd already seen. These were different. These were candid, caught from distances and angles in moments he didn't remember. She hadn't told him she was taking those pictures.

Maybe she didn't want him to know. But there he was. Him at the fence line. Him in the barn. Him at the supper table with his head turned toward someone outside the frame.

The screen door hinges squeaked, and he looked up.

Bobby stood in the kitchen doorway, her phone in one hand and the reason she'd come back was plain to see on her face. She'd forgotten her laptop, and there he was with it.

Neither spoke. She looked at the laptop screen and then at him. A blush rose to her cheeks. Her heart was in each one of those photos, and he'd just looked into it.

"I was just getting some water .. ." He didn't look away. He could have. He could have said he was sorry, but the computer was there, and he noticed his picture. He could have said something to give her a graceful exit, if only he could think of what that could be. But his mind just went blank. All he could think of was her, of the pictures, of the way she had felt in his arms when a storm raged outside, and of the place in his heart that belonged to her now. So he stood gazing and wishing he could say what he felt with the same simple truth she'd shown him with her camera.

And yet, somehow, she knew. He could see it in her eyes. It was there with the other truth they couldn't deny: it was hopeless.

His eyes flickered toward the laptop and then back at her. "I need to go check on the horses."

It was the worst excuse he'd ever given in his life,

and they both knew it. The horses were fine. He'd just walked through the barn a few minutes ago.

She took a few steps toward her laptop. He stepped aside to avoid her. He had just touched the door handle when he heard her and paused.

"Good night, Wyatt."

He turned and caught her eye. "Good night."

The door closed behind him as he took long strides toward the barn. With nothing to do there, he stood in the dark, put his hands on a stall door, and breathed.

The horses shifted in their stalls. Shadow nickered low. Wyatt put his hand on Shadow's neck and stood there until his breathing was steady again.

He wasn't sure when she'd started loving him. At the line shack, he knew. But he'd loved her before that. The first time he saw her step out of that SUV, it was like looking at the sky before a tornado. He knew something was coming; he just didn't know what. He tried to convince himself it was just an attraction. Who wouldn't, after touching that pretty ankle of hers, caught in the stirrup, want to touch more? When he did, when they danced the two-step, he knew something had changed.

But even before that, he'd watched her fall in love with the land. When she looked through that camera, her true love for the ranch that meant everything to him and his family shone through. He'd known all of this, but done nothing about it, because doing something about it meant believing that wishes come true. But that was the stuff you mucked out of a stable, not something you could build a life on. That was the business of fools.

He had been a fool once, and it cost him. Brooke taught him that.

Bobby wasn't Brooke. He knew that, too. She had worn the wrong boots, learned to ride, gotten stuck in the mud, and kept going. Never once had she complained about any of it. And one night in a storm, she gave herself to him. But none of that made a difference because she would go home.

When he was sure that she'd gone to the bunkhouse, he closed the barn door and went back to the house.

CHAPTER FIFTEEN

SHE LEFT WITHOUT THE CAMERA.

Wyatt saw her go from the barn doorway. He'd come in to check on Dolly's left fore, which she'd been favoring since Tuesday, and when he straightened up, through the open doors, he saw Bobby crossing the south pasture with her hands in her jacket pockets and nothing over her shoulder. No camera bag. No tripod. Just her, walking toward the creek in the late afternoon light with a purpose.

In two weeks he'd never once seen her go anywhere without a camera.

He watched until she dropped below the ridge and disappeared into the cedar break along the creek. Then he turned back to Dolly, lifted the hoof again, and ran his thumb along the frog but found nothing wrong with it. The horse looked at him with mild patience while he pretended to be doing something useful.

He set the hoof down. Dolly shifted her weight and went back to her hay.

Through the barn doors, the light was settling low in the sky, spreading a golden hue across the pasture grass and turning the limestone outcrops the color of honey. The live oaks threw long shadows to the east. Somewhere in the south pasture a cow called for her calf, and the calf answered. Then the evening was quiet again.

He knew where she was going. She'd gone to the same place the first afternoon she arrived, when she'd wandered down to the creek with her camera while Ruby was making supper and found the heron standing in the shallows. He'd seen her from the ridge that evening, a small figure crouched at the water's edge, shooting into the last of the light. He'd known then, before he knew anything else about her, that she saw the land the way he did.

He pulled off his gloves and hung them on the nail by the tack room door. He filled the water trough. He swept the aisle, which didn't need sweeping. He stood in the barn for ten minutes, doing nothing while the shadows on the ground grew longer.

Then, unable to help himself, he walked down to the creek.

THE TRAIL from the barn dropped through the cedar break and came out at the flat limestone shelf where the creek pooled before turning south. The water was still running high from Monday's storm, dark and clear over the gravel bed, and the pecans along the far bank were leafing out in that first pale green that meant spring had settled in for good.

Bobby was sitting on the ledge with her boots near the water and her arms around her knees. She wasn't looking at the creek. She was looking west, where the sun was dropping toward the hills and the sky was beginning to color. Her hair was down, and the light was in it.

She heard him coming and turned her head. She didn't look surprised. She didn't smile. She just watched him approach with an expression that was calm, open, and sad, and he had to look away before it broke him.

"Hey," she said.

"Hey."

He sat down beside her on the limestone, leaving a foot of space between them. Close enough to talk, but not close enough to touch. He put his forearms on his knees and looked at the water.

"Dolly okay?" she said.

"She's fine."

Bobby nodded. She looked back at the sky. Bands of peach and gold spread above the western hills, and the creek caught them and sent them back in long, shifting ribbons.

"This is where I came the first night," she said.

"I know."

"You saw me?"

"From the ridge. You were down here shooting the heron."

She turned to look at him.

She held his gaze and then looked away, down at

the water rushing over the stones. Her jaw tightened. He watched the fight happen in her shoulders, the moment she decided not to let it out.

They sat watching the creek run by them. A mockingbird was working through its repertoire in the pecan tree across the water. It went from one song into the next without pausing, and somewhere upstream a turtle slid off a log and hit the surface with a sound like a small stone dropping.

"I didn't bring my camera," she said.

"I know."

"I couldn't look at this place through a lens right now. If I put a frame around it, it would feel far away. And I'd have it to look at and remember how I'm feeling right now. I'm not ready for that." She paused.

He picked up a flat piece of limestone from beside his boot and turned it over in his hands, warm from the sun, smooth from years of water.

"Bobby."

"Don't," she said quietly, without looking at him. "If you say what I think you're going to say, I won't be able to hold it together. And I need to hold it together."

"What do you think I'm going to say?"

"That this is how it has to be."

He set the stone down on the ledge between them. "Isn't it?"

She didn't answer. The mockingbird stopped singing, and the evening was quiet except for the creek and the cattle settling in the lower pasture.

"I have a life in New York," she said. "I have clients. A lease. Work that I've spent ten years building." She said it the way someone catalogs the reasons a bridge is structurally sound while it sways underfoot.

"I know."

"And you have this." She gestured at the surrounding land, the hills, the creek, the pasture, and the sky. "You have two thousand acres that your grandfather built and your father held onto, and you'd rather die than lose. I know what this place means to you, Wyatt. I've known since the first day."

"You saw it before I showed it to you."

"That's what a photographer does."

"That's not what I mean."

She looked at him. He could see the tears she was holding back, bright in the late light. He wanted to reach for her, but he kept his hands on his knees.

"If things were different," he said.

"I like thinking about that." She tried to smile. "But they're not."

"No."

The word sat between them. He looked at the creek because looking at her face was something he couldn't do right now if he wanted to stay in one piece. The water ran over the gravel bed, the same water that had been running over this same gravel since before his grandfather found this land. The constancy of it was usually a comfort, but tonight it felt like something being taken from him.

"The subscription box is going to work," she said. "Ruby's already got some vendors lined up. And the magazine piece is strong. Kay thinks it could bring in at least two hundred orders within the first month."

He knew she was talking about the ranch because the ranch was safe ground, the place where they could be useful to each other without admitting what it meant.

"I appreciate what you've done for this family."

"Don't do that." Her voice was steady but thin, like a wire pulled too tight. "Don't thank me like I'm the contractor who fixed the barn roof."

"I wasn't."

"You were. You were putting me in a box that makes it easier to watch me leave." She turned to face him fully, and her eyes were wet, and she wasn't trying to hide it anymore. "I'm not going to make this easy for you, Wyatt. I won't pretend this was just a nice assignment in a beautiful place, because it wasn't. You know it wasn't."

He looked at her. The light was going, the gold faded to deep amber. Bobby's face in that light broke his heart. No armor, no frame to put between herself and him. Just her on the same limestone where she'd sat two weeks ago, telling him what they both already knew.

"It wasn't," he said.

Twelve inches of warm stone lay between them, close enough to bridge, and yet neither of them did.

"I think about it," he said. Words weren't his currency. He worked in land, animals, and silence, and what he felt for her wouldn't fit into any of that. But she was looking at him. "I think about what it would look like with you here. I can see it, Bobby. I can see the whole thing."

Her hand came up to her mouth.

"And I can see you giving up your life for a ranch that might not make it through the next year. I can't ask you to bet on a place that I might not hold onto. That's not fair to you."

"Don't I get a say in what's fair to me?"

"You've worked too hard to build what you've got."

She wiped her eyes with the heel of her hand. "Damn it, Wyatt. Do you think I care about the money? Do you think I care whether the ranch turns a profit next quarter? I've been a freelancer for ten years. I know what broke looks like. Broke doesn't scare me."

"It scares me."

The admission surprised even him. He wasn't a man who said such things. He'd run this ranch for seventeen years and held it close, never telling Ruby or Judd or the banker that the weight of it frightened him. But Bobby was sitting beside him, and she'd shown him her heart in a thousand pictures, and lying to her was something he couldn't manage.

She was quiet. The tears were on her face now, and she let them be there. She didn't look away from him.

"I know," she said softly.

She knew what he was telling her. It was the fear of being the Cavanaugh who lost it all, of loving her and having to ask her to lose it with him. She heard all of it and held steady.

He reached over and took her hand. Her fingers closed around his. They sat while the light left the hills. Amber fading to rose, rose to deep violet spreading east to west. The stars came out. The creek went dark, and the water sounded closer and more insistent.

He turned to her. She turned to him. In the dark, her face was all there was.

He kissed her.

It wasn't the kiss of the line shack, when the rain hammered and days of wanting broke open. This kiss was slow because they knew it was ending. He held her face in his hands and felt the tears there. He kissed her with everything he had and everything he was about to lose. Her hands found his chest, fingers gripping the fabric of his shirt as if she could keep him if she just held hard enough.

When they parted, he held her against him, his hand on her head. He held her there because the next move was letting go and he wasn't ready.

"Bobby."

"I know," she said again.

He let go.

They walked back to the house in the dark.

The trail from the creek to the barn was a quarter mile through the cedar break, and they walked it side by side without speaking. The night was clear and full of stars, and the ranch buildings were dark shapes against the sky before them except for the yellow square of the kitchen window where Ruby had left the stove light on.

The only sounds were their boots on the hard ground, the sound of the cattle settling, and the creek falling away behind them.

At the point where the trail split, left toward the bunkhouse and right toward the barn, they stopped.

The kitchen window glowed forty yards away. A coyote called from somewhere east of the property line, and a second one answered from the ridge.

He looked at her. She looked at him. What was left didn't need words.

"Good night, Wyatt."

"Good night."

She turned and walked toward the bunkhouse. He watched her go without turning back. He stood in the dark until her door opened and closed and the light came on in her window. After that, he stood there longer because moving meant the day was finished and tomorrow would be one day closer to the end.

He went to the barn, where Shadow stood at his stall door the way he always did when Wyatt came in late, ears forward, waiting. Wyatt put his hand on the horse's neck and stood amid the smell of hay, old wood, and leather saddles on the wall.

Five days.

He had five days.

He closed the barn, walked to the house, climbed the porch steps, and sat down in his father's rocker. He didn't turn on the light. He didn't go inside. He sat in the dark and looked at the bunkhouse window where her light was still on, and he sat there until it went off. Then he sat there after that, while the stars moved overhead and the coyotes sang and the creek ran on without him.

CHAPTER SIXTEEN

SHE MADE it to the bunkhouse before she fell apart. She leaned against the closed door and stood in the dark, wishing the darkness would close in around her until her heart would stop aching.

She'd managed to keep her emotions in check at the creek because falling apart in front of Wyatt Cavanaugh was something she simply would not do. But having him share those tender moments with her was too bittersweet to endure. She wondered if it might not have been better for him to push her away, to cauterize the wound, rather than prolong the agony.

From the depths of her soul came the graceless, silent tears she'd held back. She slid down to the floor, buried her face in her arms, and then sobbed until her ribs ached.

The bunkhouse was quiet. The east window was dark. Outside, the ranch had settled into its usual nighttime sounds. Cattle moaned in the lower pasture, water rushed over the rocks in the creek, and a coyote howled somewhere past the fence line. Everything was as it should be except Bobby's heart.

When she'd cried her eyes dry, she stayed on the floor because standing up meant doing something, and she just didn't care anymore. The world could just go on without her.

But after a while, she forced herself up. She couldn't have said why, except that's what she did. She got up and kept going. In the mirror over the sink, a woman stared back, looking blotchy and wrecked. She pulled her hair back, splashed cold water on her eyes, and dried her face with the hand towel. But that woman just wouldn't go away.

She sighed, grabbed her laptop, and sat on her bed because work was the answer to everything wrong with her life. It wasn't the best answer, but it would have to do for the moment. When Ted left, she edited an entire wedding's collection of photos in one day. When her mother died, she reorganized her closet by color in ROYGBIV order.

The subscription box photos needed finishing. Ruby wanted product shots for the website of the kolaches in their wrapping, the brisket rub in a cellophane bag topped with the Cavanaugh Creek label, and the miniature pecan pies she'd been testing. She'd been shooting food all week, and the images were good. Better than good. They glowed with the warmth of a country kitchen and the sense of a family that made things by hand because homemade tasted best.

She opened the folder and worked on color correction, lighting, and cropping. The mechanical rhythm of it steadied her hands, but it failed to distract her mind. She moved through the images the way she always did, making decisions with the part of her brain that operated on instinct and training while the rest of her brain did whatever it wanted, which tonight meant replaying every word Wyatt had said at the creek.

I can see the whole thing.

She adjusted the white balance on a shot of the brisket rub in its Kraft paper and moved to the next frame.

I can't ask you to bet on a place that I might not hold on to.

She cropped a close-up of Ruby's cornbread mix in its muslin bag and exported it, and opened the next one.

Her phone rang.

The screen said Kay Briggs, and the time said 10:47 p.m. Bobby tried to ignore it for two rings, but Kay didn't call this late unless she wanted something, and Bobby was fairly certain she knew what it was.

She picked up. "Hi."

"Tell me you're not asleep."

"No, I'm working."

"Good. Me too." Kay's voice had the energy it got when she had an idea she believed in. Bobby had heard that voice before the Adirondack piece, before the Hudson Valley series, before every story Kay had championed from pitch to print. It was the voice that meant she'd done her homework. "I need to talk to you about the ranch piece."

"Is there something wrong with the proofs? You said they were—"

"Gorgeous. No, it's not that. It's another piece that I've got in mind. The real one."

Bobby winced.

"I've been doing some digging," Kay said. "For family ranches in the Hill Country, the economics are devastating, Bobby. These families are getting squeezed out by import quotas, corporate packers, and drought cycles, and nobody's telling that story. Not the way it deserves to be told."

"I know."

"I talked to a county extension agent in Kerr County. And an ag economist at Texas A&M. The numbers are, I mean, these ranches are hemorrhaging. Multi-generational operations that have been running cattle since the 1940s, and they're one bad quarter away from selling to developers. It's a national story."

"Kay."

"The magazine wants it. I pitched it Tuesday and Martin is interested. A photo essay—your pictures, which are already extraordinary—paired with long-form reporting on what these families are facing. It could run eight pages."

Bobby stared at the laptop screen. A photo of Ruby's kolaches on the kitchen counter, the morning light warm on the paper wrapping. Behind them, slightly out of focus, the kitchen window framed the south pasture and the fence line running to the hills.

"You're talking about Cavanaugh Creek," Bobby said.

"I'm talking about family ranching. Cavanaugh Creek would be one example among several."

"But it would be the centerpiece. My photos are

from this ranch. The readers would know exactly where I was."

Kay was quiet for a moment. "Yes."

"And you've already looked into the family."

"I looked into the economics. The county records are public. Tax assessments, herd registrations, USDA filings. It's all out there. Anyone with a laptop can find it. I'm not doing anything underhanded."

"I didn't say you were."

"But you're thinking it."

Bobby leaned back and looked around at the bunkhouse room that had become so familiar, with its white sheets and wildflowers that Ruby refreshed every few days. This room had become a home away from home.

"Kay, these people took me in. They fed me at their table. They're good people, hardworking and proud. I can't—"

"You can't what? Report the truth?"

"I can't put their financial troubles in a magazine for the whole country to read."

"The piece wouldn't name specific dollar amounts. It would tell the story of what family ranchers are facing: the systemic pressures, the policy failures, and the human cost. That's journalism, Bobby. That's what we do."

"What you do. I take pictures."

"Don't do that. Your photos are as much a part of this story as the words are. They're what makes it work. The images you've sent me—the land, the family, the work—they're the most honest work you've done in years. You know that."

She did. And that was the problem.

"Here's what I need you to understand," Kay said as she lowered her voice into her steady businesswoman mode. "This piece is happening with or without your involvement. I just need a few photos. I can get by without them, but then you'd have no say in the framing. I thought you might like some input on which photos run and how the family is portrayed. And, you know me, I'm a collaborator."

The silence stretched. Bobby could hear the creek through the window.

"Look, Bobby," Kay added. "I'm telling you where this is going because you're my friend and because the story matters. It could actually help these families. This piece can put pressure on the quota system and draw attention to the subsidies that never reach small operators. This isn't a hit piece. It's advocacy."

"And if Wyatt doesn't see it that way?"

The question came out before Bobby could stop it, and she heard how she sounded. She'd said Wyatt—not the family, the rancher, or Mr. Cavanaugh, but his first name. And her tone had revealed how she felt about him.

Kay heard it too. "Bobby."

"Don't."

"How long?"

"Kay, this isn't—"

"What's going on?"

Bobby put her hand over her eyes. The laptop screen glowed in front of her, image after image of land she hadn't been hired to love.

"It doesn't matter," Bobby said.

"It matters a lot, actually. Because right now I don't think you're making an editorial decision. You're making a personal one. It's skewing your judgment, and you're too good to pretend that it isn't."

Bobby said nothing. Kay was right.

"Okay, it's late. Think about it," Kay said. "But I need to know by Monday. Martin's holding pages."

"Monday."

"Call me."

Bobby said she would. Kay said good night. The line went dead, and the room was quiet.

She set the phone down and sat there. She couldn't disagree with Kay's logic. Public land records. Tax assessments. USDA filings. Anyone with a laptop could find the same information Kay had found. The story was going to be published with or without Bobby. If she didn't at least try to shape it to protect what she could, someone else would. Kay would. She wouldn't mean to hurt anyone, but she would.

Kay hadn't sat at the Cavanaugh table. Kay hadn't watched Wyatt's face when he talked about what his father had built. Kay didn't know what it would cost him to see his private struggle laid open in print.

Bobby closed the laptop. She sat in the dark bunkhouse and tried to think like a journalist, but she couldn't be objective. Every argument she made circled back to the same place: a man on a limestone ledge saying I can see the whole thing.

She didn't know how long she sat there before a knock came.

RUBY WAS HOLDING A PLATE. On a small white dish were three miniature pecan pies, each one barely bigger than a silver dollar, golden-brown and glossy with a pecan half pressed into the center. Ruby's eyes were bright, and she was smiling proudly.

"Okay. Tell me these aren't the most adorable things you've ever seen." She held the plate out. "Individual pecan tarts. I used the mini muffin tin. They're still warm. Try one and tell me the pecan-to-brown-sugar ratio isn't perfect. How cute would these be in the subscription box?"

She looked from the pies up to Bobby. Her smile dropped. The plate lowered.

"Oh, honey."

Bobby shook her head. She was not going to cry again. She was done crying. She'd used up every tear in her body on the floor twenty minutes ago and there was nothing left. Except that Ruby was standing in the doorway with a plate of tiny perfect pies, and her face had gone from excitement to something so tender that Bobby's chest seized.

She lifted her chin and said brightly, "I'm fine."

Ruby set the plate on the nightstand and sat on the edge of the bed. She didn't ask what happened. She didn't push.

"Those really are adorable," Bobby said, looking at the tarts because looking at Ruby was too much.

"Bobby."

She picked up a tart and bit into it because if her mouth was full, she wouldn't have to talk. It was buttery, warm, and the pecans were toasted, and the brown sugar had caramelized into magic on a plate. "Oh, my gosh, Ruby. What have you done!"

Ruby grinned. "I think I got the ratio just right."

Bobby had almost managed to act cheerful, when her emotions spun out of control, and tears came to her eyes. She tried to smile through them, as if Ruby wouldn't notice. But from the way Ruby was eyeing her, Bobby was sure that she had. Sure that a question was coming.

But it didn't. Ruby reached over and put her hand on Bobby's. Her palm was warm and rough from work.

"I'm not blind, you know," Ruby said quietly. "I see how it is with you two."

Bobby's throat closed.

"And I see what it's costing both of you to pretend it isn't happening."

Bobby pressed her lips together and nodded. It was all she could do. If she opened her mouth, everything would come out: her feelings for Wyatt and everything else. Kay, and the story. The fact that her magazine was about to put a spotlight on Wyatt's closely held secret. She swallowed and kept it all in.

Ruby squeezed her hand once and let go. She stood up.

"Eat the tarts," she said. "There's more where that came from." A soft look came into her eyes. "You're not alone. You know that, right?"

Bobby nodded again.

Ruby left, closing the door softly behind her.

Bobby sat on the bed with a plate of pecan tarts,

surrounded by the silence of the bunkhouse. The laptop was closed on the bed. Her phone was beside it. Kay's name would top the list of recent callers. Through the window, the kitchen light glowed as Ruby walked back to the house, back to the family that had opened its door to Bobby without condition or question.

Bobby had until Monday.

She picked up another tart and ate slowly. There was no point in going to bed when she knew she wouldn't sleep.

CHAPTER SEVENTEEN

THE SILVER BMW came up the ranch road at two in the afternoon, trailing a line of caliche dust that Wyatt could see from the round pen. He was working a two-year-old gelding on the lunge line. As the horse moved in easy circles at a trot, he saw the dust plume rise above the live oaks as if weather were coming in from the west.

He knew the car before it cleared the last bend. Brooke always drove too fast on gravel.

She pulled up beside the house and stepped out of the car, wearing a cream-colored sundress and strappy heels. Her sunglasses were pushed up on her head, and her hair was a highlighted honey-blonde that cascaded down her shoulders and back. She looked exactly the way she always had: beautiful and entirely out of place.

He kept the gelding moving. The horse needed the work. So did Wyatt.

"Wyatt." She walked toward the round pen with

her arms folded and the smile she used when she wanted something. He'd been on the receiving end of it enough times to recognize it from sixty feet away.

"Brooke."

"I was in the area."

He almost smiled at that. Nobody was ever in the area of Cavanaugh Creek Ranch. The ranch sat several miles from the nearest paved road and several more miles from Kerrville. No one ended up here by chance.

"Long drive from Dallas," he said.

"I had a meeting in Fredericksburg. My father's interested in some Hill Country property."

He let the lunge line out another foot and kept his eyes on the gelding. The horse was green and didn't need distractions, and neither did Wyatt. "What can I do for you?"

She leaned against the railing. "Can we talk?"

"Sure, what's up?"

"I meant, can we go someplace and talk?"

He brought the gelding down to a walk, then to a halt. Unclipped the line. The horse stood there, blowing softly, while Wyatt coiled the rope and hung it on the rail post. He opened the gate and let the gelding into the paddock, where it dropped its head to the water trough and drank.

He turned to face her. "All right."

They walked toward the house. On the far side of the yard, Bobby was coming around the barn with her camera bag over her shoulder. She stopped when she saw them. From where Wyatt stood, he could see the exact moment she noticed Brooke and sized her up. Bobby's expression didn't change. She lifted one hand in a small wave, turned, and went in the other direction.

He felt as though he needed to explain, except there wasn't anything to explain, really. And by then, Bobby had already turned away.

THEY SAT on the front porch. Ruby brought some sweet tea because she would never let someone sit on the porch without bringing them something, even if that someone was Brooke. She smiled politely and said hello as she set the glasses down, looked sideways at Wyatt, and went back inside. The screen door closed behind her with an emphasis only Wyatt would have noticed, just as Ruby must have intended.

Brooke took a sip and set the glass on the rail. "I'll get to the point."

Wyatt waited.

"My father heard about your situation."

His stomach churned. He'd expected it, but that didn't help. He'd known it was coming from the moment the dust plume appeared above the oaks and he recognized her car. But hearing it said aloud was a punch in the gut. Someone had talked. The banker, or someone at the county office, or one of the ag guys at the co-op. It didn't matter who. What mattered was that Hank Whitfield, sitting in his corner office in a Dallas high-rise, knew that Wyatt Cavanaugh couldn't hold on to his land.

"My situation?" he said.

"Financial." She said it so easily and with such a

complete lack of awareness of his feelings that it hurt even more.

"My finances are fine."

She leveled a look. "Wyatt."

"Well, Brooke, as much as I appreciate your coming all the way out here to talk about my finances, there's really nothing to talk about."

"Wyatt, honey, there's nothing to be ashamed of. Daddy knows all about it. The back taxes, the note on the south herd. He follows the Hill Country market. He knows what family ranches are facing right now, and he wants to help."

"Your father doesn't want to help. He wants to buy, and I'm not selling."

She didn't flinch. "Well, now you're just being ornery. He's proposing a partnership. An equity stake in the ranch in exchange for enough capital to clear the debts and rebuild the herd. You'd keep operational control. Day-to-day decisions stay with you. He's not looking to run a cattle operation. He's looking to preserve one."

Wyatt looked out at the south pasture. The light was warm, and the cattle were grazing along the fence line the way they did every afternoon, drifting down toward the creek. His cattle. His fence line. His land, land that had been passed down from his father and his grandfather before him.

"No."

Her voice took on a syrupy tone. "Now, Wyatt, you haven't even heard what we're offering."

"We?"

"Well, it's Daddy's money, but it was my idea."

"Your idea? Why, did the Junior League close your chapter? Are you looking for something to fill in the void between beauty salon visits?"

A frown came and went on Brooke's face. "You shouldn't look a gift horse in the mouth."

"Now, Brooke, don't sell yourself short. You are anything but a horse. Or a gift." Wyatt tried not to scowl, but she didn't make it easy.

"Well, now you're just being unkind."

"No, I'm just being insulted." He looked sideways at her.

Brooke was clearly displeased, but she let it go and moved forward. "At least hear me out."

Wyatt waited.

"We can talk about dollar amounts later, but it would be more than enough to pay your debts—"

"My debts?"

"—rebuild the herd and infrastructure, with enough left over to carry you through the next drought without having to sell off parcels of land."

So the banker had talked. Wyatt waited for the other shoe to drop.

"And in exchange, Daddy would want thirty percent."

"Thirty percent of my ranch."

"Thirty percent of a ranch that would be solvent, which is better than a hundred percent of a ranch that isn't. Wyatt, this is a lifeline."

He picked up the iced tea and drank because if he didn't, he was going to say something he'd been raised not to say.

In the summer of 2009, when beef prices cratered,

and the drought took half the herd, his father had sat right here and told Hank Whitfield's man that Cavanaughs didn't take partners. The ranch would survive or it wouldn't, but it would do so as a Cavanaugh operation or not at all. Pop said it calmly and added, "Now drink up that tea and be on your way while I go get my shotgun."

The story was a family legend. Ruby liked to tell it at Thanksgiving.

Wyatt set the glass down. "It's a long drive from Dallas to hear me say no."

"Wyatt—"

"But that is my answer, and it's not going to change."

She was quiet. The floor creaked inside the screen door. If Wyatt were a betting man, he'd bet Ruby was standing there listening.

"Will you at least think about it?"

"I just did, You have your answer." He stood and went to the rail. Everything he saw out there was his and his family's.

Brooke got up and stood beside him. "Wyatt." If she could have frowned through the Botox, she would have. But behind that pretty pout, she was still searching for angles that she hadn't tried. She was smart and determined. When she wanted something, she found a way to get it.

She slipped her arm into his and leaned closer.

Apparently, what she wanted was him. But they'd been through this before. There was a time when he felt differently about her, but that was before he got to know her. He once thought he loved her, but she didn't love ranch life, and that was a nonnegotiable part of the deal.

"We had some good times, didn't we Wyatt?"

He didn't answer.

"I miss how we were," she said softly.

"Brooke," he turned to tell her that those days were long gone, but before he found the words, she found his mouth and kissed him.

He gripped her shoulders and stepped back until they were an arm's length apart. Then it all fell into place. "So this was your idea? Did you think you could buy me out and eventually force me to move to Dallas with you?"

Her face brightened. "We could have such a wonderful life. Wyatt, you know how I feel about you."

With a slight nod, he said, "Yeah, but you don't know how I feel about you. So let me be clear, it's over."

Her eyes narrowed almost imperceptibly. "Either way, you're going to lose it," she said.

"Maybe."

"Your grandfather built this place."

"I know who built it."

She let out an exasperated breath. "Fine, go ahead and fail, but I don't have to watch."

RUBY CAUGHT up with Brooke halfway to her car and convinced her it was too late to start driving to Dallas. She was welcome to spend the night and set off in the morning. For that, she got a scathing look from Wyatt.

"I'm sorry, but I couldn't just send her off like that."

"I could." Wyatt went out to the barn while Brooke grabbed the overnight bag she happened to have in the car.

Ruby was making pot roast for supper, which she could make in her sleep. Judd was over at Earl's, so the table was set for five.

Bobby came in from the bunkhouse at six, with her hair down, wearing jeans and a gray top. Wyatt introduced her to Brooke, which felt as awkward as anything he could remember. She sat down, put her napkin in her lap, and looked almost as uncomfortable as he felt.

Brooke watched Bobby with open curiosity. "So, you're the photographer."

"I am."

"Ruby mentioned the magazine piece. I saw the ranch on the magazine's website. They posted a preview. Your pictures are gorgeous."

"Thank you."

"How long are you here for?"

Bobby reached for the bread basket. "A few more days."

"And then back to New York?"

"That's the plan."

Brooke's smile was as pleasant as it was insincere.

Wyatt ate his pot roast and said little while Bobby looked anywhere but at him. When the silence had grown unbearably awkward, Ruby asked Wyatt how the gelding was doing. Then, to Wyatt's relief, Denny shared a story from school, which filled a good minute and a half. Bobby complimented Ruby on the meal, and everyone agreed.

After another lull, Bobby asked, "So, Brooke, you're from Dallas?"

"Born and bred."

"I've never been, but it looks amazing in the photos I've seen."

"Oh, it is!" While Brooke launched into a description of her part-time work with her father and the charity work that filled the rest of her days, that is, when she wasn't shopping. Bobby listened and nodded at all the right moments. All Wyatt could do was wonder how he found himself in this situation. And then he remembered and had a few unkind thoughts about Ruby and her hospitality. Bobby was pleasant, but he wondered if it cost her as much as it cost him to sit here and pretend that nothing was wrong.

Ruby carried more of the conversation than anyone else, describing the subscription box, a funny thing Denny had said about his science project, and how Bobby was teaching Denny about photography. Meanwhile, Wyatt sat wishing the meal would end.

After supper, Bobby helped load the dishwasher. She started to wash the pots and pans with Ruby, but Wyatt whisked Ruby away to the porch, and he grabbed a towel. Denny went upstairs to do homework, which left Brooke sitting idly at the table.

"Brooke, would you mind taking this glass of

water to Ruby?" Wyatt held out the glass. Brooke hesitated, but took it and headed outside.

Bobby was vigorously washing the dishes when Wyatt put his hand on her arm to stop her. "Bobby."

She looked at him with a distance he couldn't be imagining. "Look, I just—"

Almost as quickly as if the screen door revolved, Brooke was back, and she sat at the table.

Bobby held Wyatt's gaze for a moment, and then she went on with her work. When the last pan was dried and put away, Bobby hung the towel on the oven handle.

"I'm going to turn in," she said. "I've got an early morning. Brooke, it was nice to meet you."

"You too, Bobby."

Bobby glanced at Wyatt, "Good night."

"Night."

She left. Through the screen door, he watched her cross the yard toward the bunkhouse until her figure disappeared into the darkness.

WHEN EVERYONE else had gone upstairs to bed, Wyatt sat on the porch, grateful to be alone in the cool night air. He leaned his head back and exhaled.

Judd's pickup pulled into the driveway. He got out and, with a glance at Brooke's car, asked, "Did she go to bed?"

"Yeah."

Judd nodded and headed for the bunkhouse.

Brooke came outside and sat in the chair beside

him. She leaned closer. "I remember how we used to sit out here and talk."

Wyatt said nothing.

"That first summer. After everyone else was asleep, that was our time."

He remembered. He also remembered the morning she'd packed her car and told him she loved him but couldn't live like this anymore. That had been on this porch too.

"I miss this," she said quietly.

"Brooke."

"I know what you're going to say."

"Do you?"

She turned in the chair to face him. The porch light was off, and the only light came from the kitchen window behind and the stars overhead. In that light, her face was softer, closer to the face he'd loved five years ago in this same spot.

"Wyatt, we were so good together." She leaned forward and slipped her hand into his. "I should never have left. I know that now."

He stood and went to the railing, "That was a long time ago."

She stood and walked over to him. "Look, I know I upset you earlier, and I get it. You're under a lot of pressure. But with Daddy's money, all that pressure would be gone. You'd have room to breathe." She leaned against him and rested her hand on his chest. "And Daddy likes you, but he wants a better life for me than all this. Just think, we could have that life together."

A door closed in the bunkhouse. Footsteps crossed the yard and then stopped.

Wyatt took Brooke's wrist gently and moved her hand away from his chest.

"No," he said.

"Wyatt—"

"I'm still a rancher. Nothing's changed."

"I've changed."

"But I haven't."

The gentleness she'd been wearing fell away, and a steely resolve took its place. "You're going to regret this," she said with quiet confidence. She lifted her chin, and she meant every word. "When the bank comes for the south herd and you're selling off the last parcel of land, remember that I stood on this porch and offered you a way out."

"I'll remember."

"You're a proud man, Wyatt Cavanaugh." She looked straight at him with narrowing eyes, "But you know what they say about pride."

"At least when I fall, it'll be on my terms."

Something flickered in her eyes that reminded him of the woman he'd once loved, smart and fierce in a way he'd once admired. Even now, he couldn't say she was wrong. The pride was real. He'd inherited that, too, along with the land.

"Good night, Wyatt." She stood and walked inside. The screen door closed behind her.

He sat in the dark comforted by the constants in his life: the bright stars, the rolling hills, and the creek that ran through them.

He was thinking about turning in when he heard

footsteps crossing the driveway. For a second, he thought it might be Bobby, but he recognized Judd's uneven gait. Judd stepped up onto the porch and joined Wyatt, with his feet on the rail.

Wyatt said, "Brooke's father offered to bail us out in exchange for a 30% share in the ranch."

Judd said, "Long way to drive just to hear no."

Wyatt gave him half a nod.

Judd sat for a while, looking out at the dark the way he did when he was chewing on something. "Bobby came out to get something from the kitchen a few minutes ago. She saw that city girl with her hands on you." He let that sit. "She went back to the bunkhouse."

The air left Wyatt's lungs.

"It ain't none of my business," Judd said. "But you need to go talk to that girl. And I don't mean the one from Dallas."

He put his boots down and stood. "Night," he said, and walked back to the bunkhouse.

Wyatt stayed and sat in the darkness.

Brooke was gone by seven the next morning. He'd heard her moving through the house at six, the sound of her heels on hardwood, the guest room door closing with a firmness that spoke louder than her words. She found him in the barn, where he'd been since five. She stood in the doorway with her bag over her shoulder and the morning light behind her.

"I hope you know what you're doing," she said.

"I usually don't."

She almost smiled at that. Almost. "You're the most stubborn man I've ever known."

"That sounds about right."

"When this all falls apart, don't call me."

"I won't."

She held his gaze. Five years ago he'd loved this woman, and the fact that it hadn't worked didn't erase the two years when it did. But she thought she could make him into a man he didn't want to be so they could live a life he didn't want to have. She'd come back hoping that something had changed, but it hadn't.

"Goodbye, Wyatt."

"Brooke."

He heard the BMW start up and drive off.

Ruby appeared in the barn doorway.

"She's gone."

"For good?"

Wyatt nodded.

"Good riddance," Ruby said, and went back inside.

Wyatt looked at the gate a while longer. Then he looked at the bunkhouse, where Bobby's window was dark. She'd be out soon with her camera, the way she was every morning, steady and observant.

He went back to the horses.

CHAPTER EIGHTEEN

Bobby hadn't slept.

It wasn't for lack of trying. She'd buried herself in her quilt. Her eyes were closed, but she could still see the porch. It kept playing on a loop in her mind. Brooke Whitfield leaned the whole length of her body against Wyatt's, with her hand on his chest and her face tilted up to meet his. Bobby knew what would come next, and she wasn't about to stay to see that.

If only she hadn't forgotten her charger. But no, not only did she forget it, but she had to go back to retrieve it at just the right moment. Perfect timing. She would rather have had a dead phone than have seen what she saw.

It was dark, nearly midnight. She was halfway across the yard before she saw them on the porch. Cute couple, hot cowboy, leggy socialite, and a sad girl in the yard who would have done anything to be able to tiptoe backwards and rewind time. Instead, she just froze, then her feet started moving before her brain could decide what to do.

The walk back to the bunkhouse was a very long thirty yards in which every moment with Wyatt flashed before her eyes. Under some circumstances, those would have been treasured memories. But in this moment, the man she loved, was with another woman. So she went into the bunkhouse, slowly at first, and as soon as she felt sure Wyatt wouldn't hear her, she ran inside and smack into Judd.

"Whoa there!" He laughed as he took hold of her shoulders until she was steady. "I was just on my way to the house for a beer. Want one? Oh." He peered closer. "Are you okay?"

"Yeah," Bobby lied.

Judd scratched his head. "Are you sure? 'Cause you look kinda… not okay."

All Bobby could think of was getting into her room, but she managed to get out some words in an unsteady voice. "Oh, you know, just in a mood, I guess."

Judd nodded. "Oh, gotcha. Lady stuff."

Bobby didn't have it in her to talk anymore, so she nodded and brushed past him on her way to her room.

It was nearly dawn now. She'd spent the night staring at the ceiling as if it were a movie screen that kept playing the same movie over and over again. Brooke, with her hand on Wyatt's chest trying to do her own version of the Vulcan mind meld, if their minds were, well, not in their heads.

It wasn't as though Bobby had any claim on Wyatt. They had more or less said their goodbyes at the creek.

They'd agreed that a future together was hopeless, so she didn't have the right to feel jealous. She certainly didn't have the right to feel betrayed. She wondered if, maybe, she did have the right to feel heartbroken.

She got up when the first gray light came through the window. She got dressed, pulled on her boots, and went outside. The ranch was still. There was no light from the house and no sound from the barn. Bobby felt completely alone in the pale, pre-dawn light.

She walked to the south fence line.

She hadn't brought her camera. After last night, she didn't need to capture any more memories on this ranch. She had more than enough.

The fence line ran along the south pasture and stretched to the hills. Bobby sat on the top rail and watched the sky lighten. A few of the cattle were already up, their dark shapes moving through the mist by the creek. A mockingbird started its morning routine somewhere in the live oaks.

This wasn't exactly the way she had pictured their parting. She'd imagined a more bittersweet embrace. Well, she did get the embrace. It just wasn't with her. But Brooke was from his world. They both had that Lone Star mindset going for them. Brooke understood Texas ranch life and the codes that governed a man like Wyatt. And, of course, Brooke was beautiful and wealthy. Sometimes life wasn't fair.

But if things were different... But they weren't. So, she'd go home to New York, and life would go on. Eventually.

Who was she kidding? She loved him. She knew she loved him in the line shack, when the tornado turned and the rain drummed on the roof, and the silence between them spoke volumes because they just knew. She knew it the night she found photos of him on her laptop that weren't for the magazine story, but still she kept them. Most of all, she knew that she loved him when he came down to the creek and he kissed her goodbye. The thing about love was that sometimes it came with no warning, and you didn't have a choice. It just happened. Just like heartbreak.

A cow called from the lower pasture. Another answered. The sky turned from gray to pale gold along the eastern ridge. She would miss this.

His boots gave him away before anything else did. That particular stride on the hard ground that she'd learned to recognize without trying. Bobby didn't turn around. She just looked at the pasture and waited.

He came up beside her, where she was perched on the rail, and he leaned on the rail and looked out at the cattle and the light coming over the hills.

"Bobby."

"Morning." She was proud of how evenly she said it.

"We need to talk."

She picked at a splinter on the cedar post. "I think we said everything at the creek."

"That was before."

"Before what?"

He was quiet. She could feel him choosing his words, and the care he was taking with them made it worse. She didn't want careful. She wanted him to say whatever he was going to say so she could go pack.

"Last night," he said. "Judd told me you saw us. Brooke and me. On the porch."

"Judd told you what? I didn't tell Judd anything."

"That you saw us."

Bobby drew in a breath to protest, but she realized she'd as much as admitted it. "I forgot my charger. I didn't mean to intrude."

"I'm sorry you had to see that."

"Yeah, well, that makes two of us."

"Bobby, it's not what you think."

"What I think is it's none of my business."

This conversation was just making it worse, so Bobby turned to get down from the fence and caught her boot on the railing. She cursed at the boot as she fell. Wyatt caught her and held her. Then he whispered her name in her ear, and she was undone.

"I don't want Brooke. I want you."

The words hung between them as he held her.

He said, "What you saw was Brooke trying to rebuild something that broke long ago. She gets that now, and she's leaving today."

That should have made her feel better, and she supposed on some level it did, but then it also served as a reminder that nothing had changed. She didn't trust herself to speak. If she did, she would tell him what she couldn't admit, not to him.

"Bobby."

She raised her eyes to meet his, which turned out to be a mistake. Because she saw in his eyes the same feelings she didn't dare put in words.

Wyatt stepped back and leaned on the fence. "Brooke showed up yesterday with an offer. The thing is, I've got debts. I owe back taxes. It's not good. Her father wants to buy a thirty-percent share of the ranch. It would solve everything. But the offer came with strings attached, well, one string, Brooke. I said no."

Relief rushed through her, and then the same hopeless feeling she couldn't escape.

"The financial part," he said. "I don't talk about it outside of the family. But I thought you should know."

"You didn't have to tell me."

"I did." He set the hat on the fence post. "Because I need you to know that what I feel for you is real, even if we can't be together, and I didn't want you to leave here without knowing that."

The cattle moved along the creek down below, and the sun cleared the ridge. The morning light changed, spreading west across the limestone and grass. She was so full of love for this man and this place, and there was nothing she could do about it.

"Look at it this way. You're dodging a bullet. The ranch is in trouble," he said. "It's been in trouble for a couple of years. Drought took the herd down to 250 from 400. The Argentine import quotas undercut the feeder price so I can't rebuild. The meatpackers squeeze the margins on what's left. I've got back taxes I'm behind on and a note on the south herd that comes due in the fall, and if prices don't recover, I don't know how I'm going to cover it."

He said it plainly. No self-pity, no drama. The way a man lays out the facts when he's decided that telling the truth matters more than protecting his pride.

"This wasn't the first time Brooke's father came calling. My father sat on that porch and sent Brooke's father's man home with a glass of water and a view of his shotgun. The Cavanaughs don't sell shares of their land. That's not a business strategy. It's just who we are." He paused. "I turned Brooke's offer down because my father would have. Because this ranch is a Cavanaugh operation or it's nothing. But turning it down means I might lose the ranch."

Bobby leaned on the fence and looked at him. The man she'd watched work the land with a quiet authority she'd never seen in anyone else was standing beside her admitting the thing that scared him most. He was in danger of losing it all.

"Why are you telling me this?" she said.

"Because… I care for you, and you deserve to know who I am."

She exhaled and thought about the line shack in the rain, and his arm across her waist in the dark. She thought about the subscription box on Ruby's kitchen table, the brand she'd designed, and Judd's rub in its package. She thought about this family, this land, and this man.

"I know who you are," she said.

She met his gaze and held it.

"You belong here more than anyone who's ever set foot on this ranch," he said. "Judd knew it the first week, but we all figured it out soon enough."

She pressed her lips together. She would not cry.

"Every time I think about letting you go, I end up standing somewhere on this ranch thinking about you." A smile teased the corner of his mouth. "I don't get as much work done these days."

"Wyatt."

"I just thought you should know."

"Thank you." As she said it, it seemed so inadequate.

He nodded once.

They stood at the fence line, side by side, and watched the sun finish rising over the Hill Country. The cattle grazed. A hawk made a pass. They couldn't leave. Not yet. Wyatt covered her hand on the rail with his.

The sun climbed, and they stayed.

CHAPTER NINETEEN

THE NEXT MORNING, Bobby walked into Ruby's kitchen and found the table covered in labels and packaging.

Ruby had been up since five. Brown Kraft tags with the Cavanaugh Creek logo lay in rows across the table, sorted by product: brisket rub, kolaches, pecan tarts, jalapeño cornbread mix, and small jars of Hill Country honey. Each tag bore the ranch brand Bobby had designed two weeks ago on this same table with a Sharpie and a paper napkin. Ruby took the napkin sketch to a print shop in Kerrville and came back with five hundred adhesive tags, and they were beautiful.

"Look at this." Ruby held up one of the honey jars. The label was wrapped around it cleanly, with the photo Bobby had taken of the apiary glowing in the afternoon light. "Tell me that you wouldn't look at that and just have to taste it—you'd want it so much."

It looked like the kind of thing that showed up in a curated gift box from a holiday catalog, except that everything in it was homemade. The rub was all

Judd's, and the baked bean recipe was his, too. The honey came from his hives. The kolaches were Ruby's grandmother's recipe, and the pecan tarts were the ones Ruby had perfected last week in the mini muffin tin.

"Ruby, this is gorgeous."

Ruby grinned.

Bobby grew serious. "You realize, don't you, that once people try these sample sizes of your pecan tarts and the honey, they are going to want to order more in larger portions."

Ruby nodded and started talking about bringing in extra help when the time came. Then they moved on to vendors and timelines. Bobby sat down with her coffee and listened, taking notes and trying not to think about the fact that this was her last full day.

She'd woken that morning with Wyatt's voice in her head. "I care for you, and you deserve to know who I am." But that was a day now behind her. The sun had come up, and she had to look forward. But forward didn't look good at the moment.

She pushed those thoughts aside and focused on the labels.

By midmorning, the kitchen looked like a small-scale fulfillment center. Ruby had the first six boxes assembled on the counter, each one lined with tissue paper and carefully packed. Bobby photographed them from every angle. She shot the kolaches in their wax paper sleeves, the honey jars with the morning light coming through the window behind them, and Ruby's hands tying twine around a box.

Denny came through and grabbed a pecan tart from the cooling rack.

"Those are for the boxes," Ruby said.

"There's like forty of them," he said with a mouthful.

"Thirty-nine now."

Denny grinned and disappeared out the back door. Bobby watched him go and thought about the post-card-sized ranch photos he'd been taking for the boxes. His shot of the house through the iron gate at the entrance was in the first batch. Bobby had told him he had a good eye, and he beamed and then changed the subject, in true teenage Denny fashion.

Something from every member of this family was going into those boxes, as well as Bobby's designs and website photos. It made her feel like part of the ranch and its family, a ranch and a family she was leaving behind tomorrow.

AT NOON she went back to the bunkhouse to pack. Her suitcase was open, and the bed was covered with folded clothing, a shoe bag, and the rest of what she'd brought with her. She folded a shirt, added it to the pile, and sat down.

The wildflowers on the sill were fresh. Ruby had replaced them yesterday, the way she did every few days. Simple purple and white flowers sat in a quart-sized mason jar. The window was open, and the breeze smelled like warm grasses. Outside, the familiar sound of cattle calling to each other from the south pasture sent a wave of warmth through her. She could hear Shadow's hooves in the barn and the slow rhythm of him shifting his weight.

She was going to miss that and everything else about this place.

Her phone buzzed on the nightstand. Kay's name was on the screen.

Bobby picked it up. "Hi."

"It's me. You said Monday, and it's Monday." Kay's voice was calm, professional, and firm. "Martin is holding two pages open for the photo essay. I was thinking maybe a photo of Wyatt at his desk looking at the books. Anyway, Martin needs an answer today."

Bobby closed her eyes.

"I'm not calling to pressure you." Kay was a master at strategic, manipulative lying. "I'm calling because the piece is going to run either way, and I'd rather have you in the room shaping it than outside watching it happen."

"Kay—"

"Just listen. I've done six more Zoom interviews: extension agents, ranchers in Gillespie County and Blanco County, and an agricultural economist at A&M. The systemic picture is devastating, Bobby. These families are being squeezed out, and nobody is paying attention. This story could change that."

"I know."

"Then help me tell it."

Bobby looked at the suitcase on her bed, at the wildflowers in the jar, and at the light streaming through the east window, which made the same warm band across the quilt every afternoon.

"You don't need my photos," Bobby said.

"Come on, Bobby. You know that a picture is worth a thousand words, and it's worth a lot to me. If I'm going to tell the best version of this story, I need just a couple more photos from you. I'm thinking a group shot of some local ranchers, maybe with some Cavanaugh cattle in the background or the barn. What do you think?"

"What if I got photos of some other ranches instead of just focusing on Cavanaugh Creek?"

Kay drew a breath. "Bobby, people will get that there are other ranches involved, but sometimes the best way to tell a story like this is by putting a face on it. It's what makes stories like this relatable. Cavanaugh Creek is that face. We've already set the table, and this is our centerpiece."

"You mean Wyatt and his family are the centerpiece? Their financial situation. The back taxes. All of it. In other words, you want to make Wyatt the poster adult for failing ranches."

Kay was quiet.

"Kay, I can't."

"Bobby, think about it."

"I've thought about it. I've thought about nothing else for three days. As much as I get what you're saying, I'm sorry. The answer is no."

"Why?"

"Because these people trusted me. They let me into their home and their family, and I won't repay that by putting their private struggles in a magazine for the whole nation to see."

"Even if the story could help them?"

"Even then."

Kay exhaled. Bobby could picture her at her desk in the magazine's Midtown office, glasses pushed up on her head, a pen between her fingers. Kay was a dynamo at what she did, and she was a good person. She was right. This story mattered. That was what made it so hard, because as much as it would help Wyatt and other ranchers, it would also hurt him just as much.

"You're making a mistake," Kay said, without anger.

"Maybe."

"The piece runs regardless. I can work with the photos you've sent me. As for keeping Cavanaugh Creek Ranch out of it, county records are public. The information is there and it needs to be brought to light. Even if I were to downplay Cavanaugh Creek, other news outlets are going to pick this up."

"I know. But it won't be me, and it won't be my photos."

A long pause.

"Okay."

"Okay?"

Kay heaved a sigh.

"I disagree. But it's your call." She could hear Kay shifting gears, filing this away. "For what it's worth, I think your feelings for that rancher are clouding your judgment. I respect your decision. You have the right to be wrong."

Bobby wasn't sure what to say to that.

"Thank you?"

"Call me when you're back. We'll get lunch."

"I will. See you then."

"And Bobby? The magazine proofs are stunning. Whatever else happens, you did beautiful work."

"Thanks, Kay."

Bobby ended the call and sat on the bed. For a second, she was stunned, but then relief washed through her. It was done. She'd turned it down. Her conscience was clear. She could leave tomorrow knowing she hadn't betrayed this family.

But the relief became tangled with everything else: feelings for Wyatt, the closeness she felt to the family, the ranch, and the business she'd helped Ruby start. She was leaving them all in a difficult place that Kay's story would make even worse.

Bobby needed some air, so she stood and walked to the bunkhouse porch. The day's heat was settling in. She drew in a deep breath and looked out at the ranch. No matter how many pictures she took, she couldn't capture the fullness she felt in her heart as she took it all in.

Footsteps interrupted her thoughts. Wyatt came around the side of the bunkhouse, the side with her window. He glanced at her, and then the window. The look on his face told her everything.

He'd heard her.

How much she couldn't tell. But enough. She thought back on every word she'd said to Kay and tried to assess the damage she'd done.

You mean Wyatt and his family are the centerpiece?

Their financial situation. The back taxes. All of it. In other words, you want to make Wyatt the poster adult for failing ranches.

He stopped a few feet away and looked at her with a coldness that she'd never seen.

"Wyatt."

"I was on my way to the barn."

"I don't know what you heard, but—"

"I'm 'the poster adult for failing ranches,'" he said flatly. "That about sums it up."

"I said no."

He nodded slowly. "Yeah, I heard you say no to a story about things I told you in confidence, things I trusted you with."

"Kay came up with the idea herself. This is all the information that's out there. I mean, not about you, just in general. I wouldn't even have considered it, except shedding light on this could actually help you."

"But you considered it." His voice was so quiet and measured, it cut her to the bone.

"Well, yes, but to help you. And others. This is a nationwide issue."

He shot a pointed look. "No, this is my issue. This is my ranch. I've been running it since I was twenty. We've had hard times, but we got through them. And we didn't need some New York magazine to do it."

"Wyatt—"

"And then you show up with your camera and all your ideas. You get Ruby all excited about this business of hers. Do you really think people want to buy homemade goods once they know that they're coming from a failing ranch? That's going to hurt her, and that's on you."

"I believe in her business."

He shook his head. "You believe." He let out a soft, bitter laugh. "Well, that's all that matters, isn't it?"

"You know what I believed? I believed you—in the line shack, at the creek, at the fence line yesterday. I trusted you. And you let all that happen, and you didn't say a word." His jaw tightened. "Well, I'll give you one thing: You are good. You know how to get the story you want."

Bobby wanted to protest, but no matter what she said, it just made it worse.

Wyatt looked at her. But the man she'd come to know, the man she felt so close to, was gone. In his place was the man she'd met on that first day, strong, proud, and so distant he might as well have been a thousand miles away.

"I appreciate you turning it down," he said. "I mean that."

She didn't know what to say anymore.

"I guess that means your work here is done."

That knocked the wind out of her.

He tipped his hat, the way he had that first afternoon when she'd arrived with her suitcase and her Chelsea boots, and he walked toward the barn.

Bobby watched him. She watched his strong back and broad shoulders, and she watched the long stride that took him across the yard, through the barn door, and out of her sight.

She went inside. She refused to let her heart break

until she got back home. So she shut down her feelings and packed.

Once finished, she sat on the bed and looked at the room one last time. The wildflowers. The east window. The quilt she'd slept under for nearly three weeks. The view of the south pasture where the cattle were grazing their way toward the creek, the same as they did every afternoon, oblivious to the fact that anything had changed.

Tomorrow she'd drive to Austin, fly home to Tarrytown, and hide out in her apartment with her broken heart. In time, she'd get back to editing wedding photos, doing brand shoots, and meeting Lindsey for lunch. Somehow, they'd find a way to laugh about how deeply life sucked. Eventually, the ache in her chest would become something she could carry without it showing.

But she'd never get over Wyatt.

CHAPTER TWENTY

SHE WAS DRAGGING her spinner suitcase over the gravel to the rental car at seven in the morning when Wyatt saw her from the barn, where he'd been since five. He set down the halter he was mending and walked across the yard. He caught up with her halfway to the car, picked up the suitcase, and carried it the rest of the way. She opened the SUV hatch and stood there with her camera bag on one shoulder and her laptop bag on the other, looking as though she hadn't slept.

He hadn't either, but that wasn't anyone's problem but his.

He lifted the suitcase into the trunk and positioned it to make room for her camera bag and computer. With that done, he stepped back.

"Thank you." Her voice was softer than usual.

"Sure."

Bobby pushed the button to close the hatch, then she stood staring at the car key. Her eyes flicked toward Wyatt but never at him.

"Well…"

Ruby came out of the house with a paper sack and a travel cup. She handed both to Bobby through the driver's side window. "Kolaches and coffee for the road. You can keep the Buc-ee's travel cup."

"Ruby." Bobby's voice caught on the name.

Ruby pulled her into a hug that lasted a long time. She said something low that Wyatt couldn't hear, and Bobby nodded against her shoulder. When they let go, Ruby wiped her eyes with the back of her hand and smiled.

"Don't be a stranger. You're practically family, you know?"

Bobby started to smile, but it didn't reach her eyes.

Denny emerged from the house, hands in pockets. He extended his hand just like Wyatt had taught him, and Bobby shook it. "Keep shooting, Denny. You've got a good eye. And you've got my phone number and email if you have any questions."

Denny smiled and nodded then took a few steps back.

Judd got up from his seat on the porch and joined them. Bobby said, "Are you sure you don't want to share that brisket rub recipe? You never know, I might put a smoker on my apartment balcony."

Judd shook his head. "Ain't no way that brisket would come out right in New York." His eyes twinkled as he lifted his chin in his version of a goodbye.

Bobby turned to Wyatt. The morning light was behind her, and he couldn't read her face clearly.

"Thank you," she said. "For everything."

The words "you're welcome" got caught in his

throat, so he simply gave her a nod. Part of him wanted to say more, but there was too much to say and no time to say it. At this point, it was best not to say anything.

Bobby got in the car and started the engine. She adjusted her mirror and put on her sunglasses.

"Drive safe," he said through the open window.

Her eyes held his. It was only a second. She nodded.

The car pulled forward. Gravel crunched under the tires. She drove the ranch road the way she'd driven it that first afternoon, slow and careful past the live oaks, the limestone fence posts, and the south pasture where the cattle were grazing in the early light. He watched the car head for the gate and then sent her a text.

Gate's open, no need to get out.

She slowed down, and must have gotten the text, but she stopped anyway. She got out of the car and looked back toward the ranch. Wyatt's chest tightened. From this distance he couldn't see her face, but he knew what the ranch looked like from that spot. He'd stood there himself a thousand times. The house and the barn sat in the shade of the live oaks, the hills rose behind them, and the sky hovered above, wide and blue.

She got back in the car. It turned onto the county road and disappeared behind the cedar break, and then even the dust settled back into place.

Wyatt stood in the yard.

Ruby went inside, Judd went back to wherever

he'd been, and the ranch was quiet except for the usual sounds. A mockingbird sang its heart out in the pecan tree by the house, and the windmill by the stock tank creaked as a south wind came up.

He went to the barn and saddled Shadow.

THE BACK PASTURE stretched east from the main property along the creek's upper branch, a hundred twenty acres of rolling grass and cedar breaks bordered by Earl's land to the north and the county road to the south. It was the piece the San Antonio developer had wanted. It was the piece Wyatt's father had added to the ranch. And it was the piece Wyatt rode to when he needed to think, because nobody came out here, and the land didn't ask him questions.

Shadow picked his way along the creek bank where the recent rain had softened the ground. The water was still running higher than usual, clear over the limestone ledges, and pooling in the deeper spots where the bass held in summer. The live oaks along the bank had leafed out in the past week, filling in the canopy so the light came through dappled and green.

He rode the fence line and checked the posts and the wire the way his father had taught him, looking for sag, for rot, and places where the cedar posts had shifted in the wet ground. It was mechanical work, and it let his mind go where it wanted, which was nowhere good.

He'd said things yesterday that he couldn't take back. Some of them were true. She'd kept a secret, a secret that involved his family. She should have told him. He had a right to be angry about that.

But he may have said things that weren't fair. The line about Ruby's business. The accusation that Bobby had been working him for a story. He knew it was wrong even as he said it, but he said it anyway, because he was angry. She'd caused it, so he made her pay. Now he hated himself for it.

You are good. You know how to get the story you want.

He'd watched her face when he said it. He'd watched the words land. And yet he hadn't stopped.

Shadow snorted and sidestepped a fallen branch. Wyatt reined him around it and kept riding. The bluebonnets in the back pasture were past their peak. The ones that had been vivid blue a week ago were fading now, their petals browning at the edges. A scattering of spent blooms lay in the grass like confetti after a parade when everyone had gone home.

He rode until the sun was high and the heat settled over the land. Then he turned Shadow west toward home.

He came in through the east gate, put Shadow up, and hung the tack. He filled the water trough and forked hay into the stall, doing all of it without thinking because his hands knew the work even when his mind was somewhere on I-35 between here and Austin.

On his way to the house, he passed the bunkhouse. The door was open. Ruby must have come in to strip the bed and air the room out. He meant to keep walking, but he stopped.

He went back and looked in. The bed was made. Ruby had made it before she left, the quilt squared and the pillow centered the way she'd found it on her first day. The wildflowers were still on the sill, wilting now in the afternoon heat. Her things were gone. The room looked the way it had three weeks ago, before she showed up and changed everything.

Except she'd left something propped against the pillow.

There sat a photo in a simple wood frame. He walked over and picked it up.

It was the family at supper. Ruby was laughing, her head thrown back and her hand flat on the table, the way it got when something struck her as truly funny. Judd was mid-sentence, fork in one hand, probably stating some bit of country philosophy as no one but Judd could. Denny was reaching across for the cornbread basket with the casual obliviousness of a teenager whose life centered on photos and food, but not in that order.

And Wyatt. He was at the head of the table, turned slightly to his left, looking at someone just outside the frame. The expression on his face was one he had never seen on himself: unguarded and warm. It was a portrait of a man who didn't have a clue that he was falling in love.

Hank's Camera Shop was stamped on the frame's backing paper.

He sat down on the edge of the bunk. Her bunk. He could still smell her in the room, a soft floral scent that was hers alone. He held the photograph and looked at it.

They were all together in their most ordinary setting, at home, having supper. And the woman who had understood the importance of that enough to capture it in a photo was on her way home to New York.

"Oh."

Ruby stood in the doorway with an empty laundry basket on her hip. She'd apparently come to strip the bed. But seeing him with the photograph in his hands, she set the basket on the floor.

She walked over and sat beside him, where she studied the photo.

"That girl," Ruby said quietly.

Wyatt said nothing.

Ruby straightened up. She looked at him with the expression she'd been giving him since she was old enough to know he was making a mistake and too kind to say it outright. But today she wasn't being kind. Today, she was being Ruby and, if Wyatt knew her, she was about to unleash some hard truths that would sting.

"Her plane leaves at six."

He looked at the window. The afternoon light slanted through the glass, casting a long gold band across the wide-planked wood floor.

"It's a three-hour drive to Austin," Ruby added. As if he didn't know.

"I'm not chasing her to the airport."

"Why not?"

"Because it doesn't fix anything. She kept something from me. She had a week to tell me, and she didn't."

"She turned it down."

"I know she turned it down. Wait. She told you?"

"Of course she told me. And you told her that her work here was done. So she left. Because you sent her away."

He looked at his sister. Ruby held his gaze without blinking. She had their mother's eyes and their father's stubbornness, and right now both were aimed directly at him.

"You told that woman she was finished here," Ruby said. "After everything she did for this family—the business plan, the brand, the website, and those pictures of hers. Our ranch is going to be in a magazine, and that's going to help us. But you sent her away because you didn't get your way."

"She broke my trust."

"She protected your trust. She turned the story down. You heard her yourself when you were lurking outside of her window."

"I wasn't lurking. I walked by and she called my name. Don't tell me you wouldn't listen."

"Well, apparently you didn't listen well enough because all that time she took deciding, which you got so angry about, was because she was trying to find a way to help us."

Ruby picked up the laundry basket. "I'm wasting my time. I love you, Wyatt, but you are the most stubborn man who ever drew breath on this ranch, and that includes Daddy, Granddaddy, and every ornery bull we've ever owned."

She walked out.

Wyatt sat on the bunk with the photo in his hands. The room was quiet. The wilting flowers on the sill caught the afternoon light, and somewhere outside a dove called from the fence line.

Ruby was right. She had a bad habit of that.

But that didn't mean that chasing after her would solve anything. That wasn't who he was. Cavanaughs didn't chase. Cavanaughs held the land and waited for the world to come to them, and when it didn't, they tipped their hats and went back to work. His father had been that way. His grandfather. The whole stubborn, proud, lonely line of them.

Besides, if he followed Ruby's advice and drove to Austin, she'd be at the gate by the time he arrived. He wouldn't get to the gate unless he bought a ticket. Assuming he had money to throw away on plane tickets that he wouldn't use, what did Ruby expect him to do then? He wouldn't have time to undo what he said yesterday. He'd probably just have enough time to tell her the truth about how he felt. He could see it already. She would slap him in the face, turn, and march onto the plane in her cute little ropers.

If for some reason she actually believed him and even more miraculously forgave him, they would be back at the fence again, realizing that it couldn't work. In a way, maybe it was easier to let her just hate him. She'd get over him faster. He wouldn't get over her, but getting over her was never going to be an option. Maybe letting her go was the kind thing to do.

He sat there.

Judd's footsteps approached in the hallway. He paused in the doorway, his usual unhurried self.

"So… y'all gonna let that one drive away too?" He didn't wait for an answer. The footsteps continued out the door.

Wyatt closed his eyes.

He sat there doing something completely uncharacteristic. He just sat and did nothing, because once he got up, he'd have to start living with what he had done.

CHAPTER TWENTY-ONE

Bobby came through the door with two bags of groceries and set them on the kitchen counter. Milk, eggs, the good sourdough from the bakery on Main Street, and a rotisserie chicken she'd pick at for three days. Tuesday errands. Tuesday life.

She'd been back in Tarrytown for seventeen days.

The apartment was a one-bedroom on the second floor of a converted Victorian, close enough to the train station that she could hear the Metro-North come and go if the windows were open. She'd loved it when she signed the lease four years ago. It had good light in the mornings, a claw-foot tub in the bathroom, and a landlord who left her alone. Now it felt small. Not just the apartment. Everything felt smaller since she'd come back. The streets, the river, the sky. She'd spent three weeks under a sky that went on forever, and Tarrytown's version looked like someone had pulled the ceiling down a few feet.

She'd been shooting again. Two weddings since

she got home, a bridal portrait session, and an inquiry about a corporate headshot package she would probably take because the rent didn't care about her feelings. The work was fine. She was fine. She kept telling people that until it almost sounded true.

The FedEx envelope was leaning against the door when she'd come up the stairs, and she'd tucked it under her arm with the groceries. Now she picked it up from the counter and looked at the label. Kay's assistant's handwriting. She leaned against the counter and opened it.

It was the magazine spread. Six pages, full bleed. The cover line read The Last Cattlemen: Life on a Texas Hill Country Ranch. One of her photos was beneath it, with the limestone house at the end of the live oak-lined lane as the late afternoon light turned the stone to gold. She turned the pages slowly. The smoker at dawn, the cattle at the creek, Ruby's kitchen table set for supper, and the overhead shot she'd taken from a stepladder while Ruby laughed and told her she was going to fall and break her neck.

Kay's sticky note was on the inside cover:

One of the best pieces we've published this year. Congratulations. Call me when you're ready to talk about what's next. –K

Bobby held the magazine in both hands and looked at it. It was beautiful. She was proud of the work. She could see that with the part of her brain that still functioned as a professional. The composition was strong, the color was rich, and she'd captured something real about that place and those people that many assignment photographers would have missed.

She should have felt more than she did.

She set the magazine on the kitchen table, went to the couch, and opened her laptop.

The plan was to respond to Kay, organize the magazine files into the archive folder—she hadn't been ready to archive them yet—and then get to work on the latest wedding proofs, which were sitting in her hard drive like a surly collection of photos she didn't want to deal with right now.

She used to be organized and on top of her workload, not spending two weeks of her life gazing into the distance while memories kept reminding her that her heart ached.

She opened the photo library, clicked on the archive folder, and then, because her fingers apparently operated independently of her judgment, she clicked on the folder labeled "Texas: Personal."

She told herself she was archiving. Organizing. Doing the responsible thing by sorting these into proper subfolders so they weren't just sitting in a heap on her hard drive, taking up space. This was professional housekeeping. It was fine.

She was not fine.

The first photos were from the early days, the ones that still felt safe: the gate and the ranch road, the live oaks making a canopy overhead, the bunkhouse window at dawn. The wildflowers on the sill that Ruby had put there before Bobby arrived, which Bobby didn't know until later, when Ruby mentioned it offhand like it was nothing, like making a stranger's room beautiful was just what you did.

She kept scrolling.

The smoker at five in the morning, Judd's silhouette against the glow of the firebox. She'd gotten up before dawn to catch that shot, and Judd had looked at her for a long time before he said anything. Then he'd handed her a cup of coffee and told her where to stand so the smoke wouldn't blow in her lens. That was the morning he'd said, "Seven spices," and walked away, and she'd laughed so hard she almost dropped her camera.

The rodeo. Denny was competing in the junior roping, his face tight with concentration, looking so much like his uncle that it made her heart ache. The grand entry flags. The dust rising from the warm-up arena in the late-afternoon light. Ruby and Diego in the stands, sitting close enough that their shoulders touched, both of them pretending they didn't notice.

The dance. She didn't have many photos there because she'd been on the floor having too much fun learning to do the two-step. But she had one from earlier that evening, taken at the bar before the music started. Wyatt was leaning against the rail with a longneck in one hand, talking to someone out of frame, and he was almost smiling. Not quite. Just the corner of his mouth and a softness around his eyes that most people would have missed. She hadn't missed it. She'd taken the photo from across the room without thinking, the way you reach for a light switch in the dark.

The line shack.

She'd taken one photo that morning before they

left for home. The light was coming through the single window, gray and rain-washed, and it fell across the narrow cot and the woodstove. His hat hung on the hook by the door. His boots lay on the floor where he'd left them. The cot was rumpled and warm, and she could still feel the shape of the night in the room, in the stillness, in the way the air smelled like cedar smoke and rain.

She looked at that photo for a long time.

The creek. The afternoon he'd found her there, the spot where she'd gone on her very first day, the limestone ledge and the water running clear over the rocks. She'd taken a few shots of the light on the water before he showed up. She supposed they were technically excellent, but all she cared about was what happened next. She remembered that kiss. She could feel his lips on hers. They'd lost the urgent desire of the line shack. This kiss was just sad and final. She remembered walking back in the dark beside him, and the feel of his hand holding hers.

And then him. Just him. The candids she'd taken without deciding to take them, the ones she'd found on her camera like evidence of a crime she didn't remember committing. She could make a photo album of falling in love from those pictures. Wyatt at the fence line. Wyatt in the barn doorway. Wyatt at the head of the supper table, turned toward her with an expression that made her want to climb through the screen and back into that kitchen where Ruby was laughing, Judd was holding court, and Denny was reaching for the cornbread. Everything was just right.

The screen blurred.

She took off her glasses and wiped her eyes with the back of her hand, which didn't help because more tears came to replace them. These were tears from a bottomless well.

She closed the laptop.

For a while, she just sat there, hands on the closed lid, breathing. Outside, a car horn honked on Main Street, and someone's dog barked twice and stopped. The radiator clicked. The apartment was so quiet she could hear the refrigerator humming.

She picked up her phone and texted Lindsey.

Lunch at the diner?

The reply came in four seconds.

I can be there by noon.

Bobby looked at the text. She hadn't told Lindsey anything was wrong. She hadn't told Lindsey anything at all, really, beyond the basics: she was back, she was working, she was fine. But, knowing Lindsey, she'd been waiting for this text. She would have known it was coming because she was that kind of friend.

THE DINER WAS three blocks from Bobby's apartment, a narrow place with red leather booths and coffee that arrived almost before you could sit down. Bobby had been coming here since moving to Tarrytown. The waitstaff all knew her.

Lindsey was already in a booth by the window. She had two glasses of white wine in front of her and slid one to Bobby with a look on her face that said she was in it for the duration if need be.

Bobby sat down across from her and slid the menu aside. She knew what she was going to order.

"Hi," Lindsey said.

"Hi."

Lindsey waited, eyebrows raised.

Bobby put the menu down. "I'm fine."

"You are not fine."

"I'm mostly fine."

"You look like you've been crying."

"I have allergies."

"You don't have allergies."

"Maybe I developed them in Texas."

"You developed something in Texas, and it wasn't just photos."

Bobby looked at her best friend across the table. Lindsey had her dark hair pulled back, she was wearing a long-sleeved T-shirt, and an expression so kind that Bobby almost lost it right there in the diner.

"The magazine spread came today," Bobby said.

"And?"

"It's beautiful. It's some of the best work I've ever done."

"And?"

Bobby picked up a piece of bread and tore it in half. "And I sat on my couch looking at photos that never made it to the magazine because they were of him."

"Hold it right there. That's the part that you tend to leave out, and I want to know more. So let's have some gut spilling. But don't make a mess," Lindsey said.

Bobby looked down at the napkin she hadn't realized she was tearing into tiny pieces. "His name's Wyatt, and he owns the ranch. And... we had feelings."

Lindsey narrowed her eyes. "Feelings? Like I feel like I'm coming down with a cold kind of feelings, or I feel like having a burger for lunch, or I feel like hopping into his saddle and—"

"That one. And I did. And we felt all the feelings, including the ones where you have to say goodbye, and you know you'll never feel like that for anyone else for the rest of your life." Bobby dabbed her eyes with what was left of her napkin.

"I figured as much."

"How? I never even mentioned his name."

"Which is so not you, Bobby. And that's how I knew."

What could have turned into an unabashed sobbing session was narrowly averted by the arrival of their food. Lindsey took a bite from her burger and said, "I'll bet they don't have New York diner food like this in Texas."

"No, but they've got brisket."

Lindsey looked at Bobby, confused, as tears welled up in Bobby's eyes. "Yeah, well, brisket's an emotional food."

Bobby said, "And I made the mistake of going through photos of him that I'd taken. I guess I thought if I archived the photos, I could archive my feelings."

Lindsey didn't look surprised. "I'm pretty sure that's not how it works."

Bobby nodded. "Yeah, but it should, don't you think?"

"Absolutely." She smiled the same understanding smile Bobby had known since they shared a one-bedroom apartment in Astoria three blocks from the elevated subway stop.

"Tell me about him," Lindsey said.

So Bobby told her. Not all of it. Not the details of the line shack. That belonged to her and Wyatt, and a tin roof in the rain. She gave her the highlights: the ranch, the family, Judd's smoker, Ruby's kitchen, and the business plan they'd built together. The two-step. The creek.

And then she came to the hard part. The way he'd said, "Your work here is done," and she knew that she'd lost him. He'd heard the wrong part of a phone call with Kay, and his pride was as wide as the distance between Tarrytown and Texas.

Lindsey listened without interrupting. She ate bread. She sipped her wine. When Bobby was done, she was quiet for a few seconds, which was unusual for Lindsey, who generally exhaled opinions the way other people exhaled carbon dioxide.

"Can I say something?" Lindsey said.

"I have never known you to ask for permission." Bobby attempted a smile.

"The last time I saw you light up like this about a man was last… never."

Bobby's brows drew together. She was pretty sure that's what she'd been trying to explain.

Lindsey dipped a French fry in a blob of ketchup and continued, "When you called me from that ranch, we were chatting like we do. The weather's hot. Spring's in full bloom. And then I asked you about the ranch owner, and you went so quiet I thought the call dropped. You have never in your life gone radio silent about a man, Bobby. A few seconds later, you started talking about the light and how amazing it was, at which point, I thought we were speaking in code, and 'light' was the code word for 'cowboy's butt in Wranglers'."

Bobby stared at her bread and muttered, "That tracks."

Lindsey thought for a moment. "So I'm trying to figure out the downside of this. You're crazy about him; he's crazy about you."

"Was." She looked at the plate of food she had no appetite for. "The damage was too deep, but even if he didn't hate me and never wanted to see me again, there was no hope for us to begin with. Our lives are too different. It wasn't meant to be." Bobby shrugged hopelessly.

For the first time since their food had arrived, Lindsey set down her fork. "Don't give me that 'meant to be' crap." People make choices. And before you say anything, people have disagreements, but that doesn't mean it's forever.

"He doesn't want to hear from me."

"You don't know that."

"Uh, yeah, I do, because he told me so, more or less."

"He was hurt. People say stupid things when they're hurt. You once told me my makeup looked a bit off, and I still haven't fully recovered."

"You'd just been caught in a rainstorm! Your eye makeup ran. You look like the Joker. But because I'm such a good friend, I didn't tell you that part." Bobby would have laughed if her life wasn't falling apart.

Lindsey said, "My point is... What was my point? Oh yeah. Love conquers all?"

Bobby rolled her eyes. "Is that the best you've got?"

"On short notice. But I'll work up some new material for next time."

"In the meantime, what do I do?" Bobby sighed and stared out the window.

Lindsey picked up her wine glass. "I think you already know."

"If I knew, I wouldn't be here."

"You've still got to eat, so you're welcome."

Having exhausted the topic of her miserable love life, Bobby changed the subject. Lindsey's sister's new baby was adorable. The super hadn't fixed the leak in her bathroom, so Lindsey bought some of that tape from TV to seal off the pipes. When they got to counting the number of Jane Austen adaptations to date, they decided it was time for the check.

By the time Bobby walked out into the cloudy spring afternoon, she felt something she hadn't felt in seventeen days, a tiny step closer to normal.

Lindsey hugged her on the sidewalk. "Don't forget to write."

Bobby managed a laugh.

"I mean it. Call me."

"I will."

Lindsey looked at her for a second longer than necessary, then squeezed her arm and walked to her car.

ONCE HOME, Bobby set her purse on the tiny half-circular table by the door, glanced at her laptop, and decided to leave it there, closed.

The magazine was on the kitchen table. She looked at it, chose not to open it, and reread Kay's sticky note.

Call me when you're ready to talk about what's next.

What was next? She didn't know. But whatever work Kay threw her way would be welcomed as long as it didn't involve hopelessly falling in love. She didn't know if the ache in her chest was ever going to fade into the background the way it needed to if she was ever to function as a normal human again.

She sat down on the couch.

Her phone was in her hand. She didn't remember picking it up.

She looked at it, scrolled to his name, and read his last text from her last morning there.

Gate's open, no need to get out.

The fact that she'd saved such a ridiculously

mundane text message spoke volumes for where her heart was, which was not a good place.

She stared at his name on the screen. Her thumb hovered over the call button. One tap. That was all it would take. One tap and she'd hear his voice. But then she'd have to say something, and she didn't have anything to say that would fix what was broken.

She'd already told him that she'd turned the story down. She'd chosen to protect him at least as much as she could. Too bad it wasn't enough.

She set the phone face down on the couch cushion beside her.

CHAPTER TWENTY-TWO

ON A SATURDAY MORNING in late April, the windows were open for the first time since she'd come home. The magnolia in the front yard had bloomed overnight, and a sweet scent wafted through her apartment. She was sitting cross-legged on the couch with her laptop, color-correcting photographs of a bride and groom whose names she'd had to look up twice on the contract. The bride had wanted photos at the Tarrytown Lighthouse, while the groom was more interested in the bar. She made them both look like they were exactly where they wanted to be. Lately, she'd wondered how this kind of love could ever last.

She'd been back from Texas for five weeks.

Five weeks. It sounded like a reasonable amount of time. People recovered from broken bones in five weeks or bad haircuts. As for ill-advised trips to cattle ranches in the Texas Hill Country, those only worked if you didn't fall in love.

In the past five weeks, she'd photographed another

wedding, taken headshots for a law firm in White Plains, and done a product shoot for a candle company that wanted everything to look "rustic but elevated." She'd said yes to every job that came in because empty afternoons didn't tend to go well. Empty afternoons led to pining and wondering what if.

She'd been emailing with Ruby about vendors, packaging, and shipping logistics for the subscription boxes. Ruby's emails were warm, detailed, and scrupulously free of any mention of her brother. Bobby's replies were the same, as if they'd made an unwritten pact to avoid talk of Wyatt. The business was neutral ground. Bobby would help build it from twelve hundred miles away because she'd promised and because it mattered. It was helping the family, and that was the one thread she couldn't bring herself to cut.

It wasn't as though she didn't want to ask about Wyatt. She just didn't, because she just couldn't. Ruby didn't volunteer.

The magazine spread was still on her kitchen table. She'd moved it to the bookshelf once, then to the desk, then back to the table. His last text was still in her phone.

Gate's open, no need to get out.

She kept looking at it as if something might change, and because he'd sent it to her. She shook her head and blinked back threatening tears. They didn't come as often, but they stung just as much.

The knock came again. Louder.

She set the laptop aside and went to the door. Lindsey always texted first. The exterminator had been there a week before, and she was pretty sure she hadn't ordered anything from Amazon. But sometimes she forgot.

She brushed back some stray strands of hair, turned the deadbolt, and opened the door.

Wyatt Cavanaugh.

Wyatt Cavanaugh was standing in her hallway.

She stared.

He was holding a cardboard box printed with the Cavanaugh Creek logo she'd designed. He was wearing his good boots, the alligator boots with the scrollwork on top. He wasn't wearing his hat, but he had on a dark blue pearl-snap shirt that looked new. At least she'd never seen it before. It looked good on him because everything looked good on him. He looked desperately uncomfortable, at which point she realized she hadn't said a word. She had just left him standing outside her door.

"I was in the neighborhood," he said. Then his face lit up with a bashful grin, the sight of which sent warmth rushing through her until she thought she might swoon.

Bobby stood in the doorway with one hand on the knob. Everything she wished she had said over the past several weeks vaporized on the spot.

"You're here," she said. It was the best she could do.

"I'm here."

"You hate flying."

"I don't love it."

He shifted the box in his arms.

"Would you mind if I set this down? It's getting kind of heavy."

She stepped back and gestured for him to come in. He set the box on her kitchen table, right next to the magazine spread with his ranch on the cover.

He looked around the apartment. She watched him take in the small kitchen, the claw-foot tub visible through the bathroom door, the couch with her laptop and the throw pillows, and the window with the magnolia tree outside. He was seeing her life, the one she'd come back to. The one she kept telling people was fine.

"Nice place," he said.

"Thanks."

"It's small."

"It's New York."

Bobby looked at the box. Brown cardboard, neatly taped. A shipping label in Ruby's handwriting, addressed to Bobby Tapley. She could feel her composure, which she'd been maintaining for five weeks through sheer force of will, starting to give.

"So this is it?"

"Yes, ma'am."

She stopped walking. "So… you're working for FedEx now?"

"We thought you should get the first one."

Bobby smiled to hide the emotion welling up inside her.

"Aren't you going to open it?" he said.

"Yes!" She carefully pulled the tape off and folded

back the flaps. Tissue paper, white and clean, packed with care. She pushed it aside.

The first thing she saw was the label. Bobby's Cavanaugh Creek Ranch logo, the one Bobby had sketched on a paper napkin at the kitchen table while Ruby heated water for coffee. The logo was on everything in the box, simple, rustic, and perfect. The brand they'd built together at that kitchen table was here, in Bobby's kitchen, twelve hundred miles from where they'd dreamed it up.

She lifted out a clear cellophane bag fastened at the top with a folded cardboard label. Judd's Dry Rub. Underneath that, it said "Seven Spices. Don't Ask."

Bobby laughed. "That last part's new."

"Judd insisted on the 'Don't Ask' part," Wyatt said. "Ruby tried to talk him out of it, but he told her he was fixin' to shut down the whole operation if she didn't agree to it."

She set down Judd's Dry Rub, reached in again, and pulled out a jar of Hill Country honey that shone amber in the morning light from the window. Her photo of the apiary was on the label. She set the jar down carefully.

Next was a small muslin pouch of jalapeño cornbread mix with a handwritten recipe card tied with string at the top.

In a small cardboard box with a cellophane window were two pecan tarts. Bobby remembered the morning Ruby had brought her a plate of prototypes. *Try these and tell me which one you'd pay for.*

On top of the cold packs were Ruby's sausage kolaches in a wax paper sleeve sealed with a

Cavanaugh Creek sticker. It put her right back in Ruby's kitchen with flour on the table and Ruby's voice telling her to fold, not press, the dough. And last was Judd's brisket surrounded by dry ice packs.

She lined all the items on the table, one by one, next to the magazine. Every item was a piece of someone she loved. Judd's stubbornness and thirty years of smoker wisdom. Ruby's warmth and her grandmother's recipes in every kolache, every bit of cornbread mix, every handwritten note. Bobby's own photographs on every label, looking back at her from a distance she had not figured out how to close.

And at the bottom, a postcard-sized photograph. She picked it up and turned it over.

The heron at the creek. Standing in the shallow water, the limestone ledge behind it, the live oaks reflected in the still places where the current slowed. Denny's photograph. The one she'd told him was his best work, and he'd grinned and changed the subject the way fifteen-year-olds do when sincerity comes at them faster than they can handle.

Bobby stood at her kitchen table holding a photograph taken by a boy she loved like family. Five weeks of holding it together came apart. She lost the fight she'd been winning since she opened the door.

She didn't make a sound, and she couldn't look at Wyatt. She just stood there with Denny's photograph in her hand, tears running down her face, and a hush in the room that was different from the silence of the last five weeks, because Wyatt was in it.

"Bobby." His voice was close. He'd come around the table.

She shook her head. Her voice wasn't going to work yet.

"I was wrong," he said. "About the story. About your work being done. About us being done." He took a breath that she could see cost him. "You turned down a story that could help other ranchers to protect my family. I repaid that by sending you home."

"Wyatt—"

"Let me finish. I practiced this the whole way here on the plane, and I'm gonna get it right."

She pressed her lips together.

"Ruby told me everything. The calls from Kay. The pressure you were under. How you said no before I ever overheard you, and said no again after, and never once wavered." He stopped. "And then she told me I was the most stubborn man who ever drew breath on that ranch, and that includes our daddy, our granddaddy, and every ornery bull we've ever owned."

Bobby made a sound that was half laugh, half sob.

"Judd said I was a fool. He didn't feel the need to elaborate. And Denny left a note on my truck that said, 'Two words: Tell her.' He gets his wordiness from my side of the family."

"Wyatt."

"I love you." He said it simply and directly. "I should have told you at the creek. I should have told you at the fence line. I should have said it the morning you left, but I didn't, because I was too proud and too scared to believe that a man who can barely keep his ranch out of the red had any right to ask a woman like you to stay."

Bobby wiped her eyes with the back of her hand.

"There's one more thing that you missed," he said quietly. He nodded toward the box.

She looked inside. Tucked in the corner, half hidden under the tissue paper, was a small package wrapped in brown paper and tied with twine. A sprig of dried wildflowers was tucked under the string, the same purple and white flowers Ruby put on the bunkhouse windowsill every few days, the ones that had been there when Bobby arrived and were wilting when she left.

She picked it up. It weighed almost nothing. She pulled the twine loose and unfolded the paper.

A ring.

A slender gold band with a small, clear stone. It wasn't flashy. It was simple and perfect.

He said, "It was my mother's."

She looked up at him.

Wyatt was watching her with the expression she'd seen once before in the photograph she'd left propped against the bunkhouse pillow. Unguarded and warm. Also terrified.

The ring was warm in her palm.

"I'm not a rancher," she said.

"I know."

"I'm a photographer."

"The ranch needs one."

She looked at the ring in her hand. She looked at the box on the table, and she looked at the man who'd flown all the way here because he wasn't one for speeches, but he knew how to show up.

"Could you see yourself living on a ranch?" he said.

Bobby thought about her apartment, the claw-foot tub, the Metro-North at night, the coffee shop on Main Street three blocks away, the site of so many heart-to-heart talks with Lindsey. She saw the limestone house at the end of the live oaks, the east-facing window in the bunkhouse, Ruby's kitchen, Judd's smoker, Denny's photographs, and the creek running over limestone in the late light. She could see the back pasture at dawn, when the sky was so wide it made her chest ache, and the stars in the night sky that went on forever in every direction. There were so many that the first time she'd seen them, she stood in the dark with her camera forgotten in her hand and just looked.

She thought about the tin roof in the rain and Wyatt's arms around her.

"I'll go pack my bags," she said as she looked up at him.

"Not yet." He got down on one knee and gestured toward the ring in her hand. "Aren't you going to put that thing on?"

She smiled and held out the ring. "You do it."

He began to, then stopped. "Just so we're clear, you're agreeing to marry me, right?"

Bobby laughed. "Yes! I am absolutely agreeing to marry you!"

Wyatt slid the ring on, then stood, lifted her off the ground, and spun her around. Then he kissed her in her small apartment where the magnolia bloomed outside her window, and the Hudson glinted through the trees.

And she kissed him again, because she was going home.

EPILOGUE

SUNLIGHT CAME through the live oaks and hit the limestone and the creek, turning the whole world into something worth getting up at dawn for.

Bobby knew this light now.

She could find the angle at dawn when the mist burned off the creek and cattle moved along the bank. She knew when the evening light would descend low and warm through the cedars and turn the limestone house the color of honey. She knew the look of the sky before a storm, and the sound of a south wind moving through live oaks.

She'd been back at Cavanaugh Creek for three months. Long enough that the bunkhouse wasn't hers anymore. She'd moved into the main house.

The magazine piece had done what Bobby always hoped it would do. Two hundred subscription orders came in during the first month alone. The Cavanaugh Creek website, with Bobby's design, photos, and Ruby's words, just kept bringing in orders. Judd's brisket sold out. Ruby cried. Judd just squinted at the order screen and said, "Huh."

Bobby was in the back pasture with her camera and a thermos of Ruby's coffee, shooting the creek before the cattle came down to water. The summer grass was high, gold and green, and the live oaks along the bank threw long shadows that shifted with the breeze. The ring on her left hand caught the early light every time she adjusted the lens.

She'd shot half a dozen frames when she heard Shadow's hooves. She pivoted, pointed her camera at the approaching silhouette, and took the shot. She had photographed this man a hundred times and not gotten tired of it.

He caught her.

"Were you going to tell me?" he said, walking Shadow over.

"Tell you what?"

"That you were pointing that thing at me again."

"I was photographing the creek. You rode into the frame. That's your problem, not mine."

He swung down from the saddle. Shadow dropped his head to the grass. Wyatt walked over with the almost smile that she loved.

He reached for the camera.

"What are you doing?"

"Borrowing this."

"That camera costs more than your saddle."

"I'll be gentle."

She let him take it. He turned it and pointed it at her. She heard the shutter.

"You don't need that right now," he said, and took another frame before she could argue.

She stood in the pasture in morning light wearing ropers, jeans, and a T-shirt, with coffee in one hand and the other hand raised in surrender. He photographed her the way she'd been photographing him all summer, as if she was all that mattered and always had been.

"Let me see," she said.

He handed it back. She looked at the screen. She was squinting and laughing, her hair loose, her face unguarded. The pasture stretched behind her to the hills, and the sky went on forever. She looked like a woman who lived here. She looked like she belonged.

She held it up and turned it so both of them were in the frame, with her cheek against his and her arm extended at a hopeless angle that made no sense.

"This is ridiculous," he said.

"Hold still."

She took the photo.

It was off center, slightly blurred, with the top of his hat cropped off and her eyes half-closed as she grinned. This was her new favorite photo because his arm was around her, the ranch was behind them, and the look in his eyes was unguarded, warm, and completely in love. As for her, it was a portrait of the artist at home.

THANK YOU!

Thank you for reading! If you enjoyed this book, please consider leaving a review or a rating. Your feedback on bookstore, Goodreads, and Bookbub websites helps other readers discover books they'll enjoy.

instagram.com/jljarvis.writer
facebook.com/jljarvis1writer
x.com/JLJarvis_writer
youtube.com/@jljarvis-author
goodreads.com/jljarvis
bookbub.com/authors/j-l-jarvis

ALSO BY J.L. JARVIS

Waterfront Summers

(Can be read in any order)

The Cottage at Peregrine Cove

The House on Serenity Lake

Moonlight on Mariner's Bluff

Drake & Wilde Mysteries

(Reading Order)

Love in the Time of Pumpkins

Secrets in the Hollow

Shadow of the Horseman

Standalones

(Can be read in any order)

A Cowboy Kind of Love

A Christmas Eve Stop

Christmas by Lamplight

A Kiss in the Rain

App-ily Ever After

Once Upon a Winter

The Red Rose

Highland Vow

Short Stories

(Can be read in any order)

The Magic of Snow

The Eleventh-Hour Pact

A Christmas Yarn

The Farmer and the Belle

Work-Crush Balance

Cedar Creek

(Can be read in any order)

Christmas at Cedar Creek

Snowstorm at Cedar Creek

Sunlight on Cedar Creek

Pine Harbor

(Reading Order)

Allison's Pine Harbor Summer

Evelyn's Pine Harbor Autumn

Lydia's Pine Harbor Christmas

Holiday House

(Can be read in any order)

The Christmas Cabin

The Winter Lodge

The Lighthouse

The Christmas Castle

The Beach House

The Christmas Tree Inn

The Holiday Hideaway

Highland Passage

(Can be read in any order)

Highland Passage

Knight Errant

Lost Bride

Highland Soldiers

(Reading Order)

The Enemy

The Betrayal

The Return

The Wanderer

American Hearts

(Can be read in any order)

Secret Hearts

Forbidden Hearts

Runaway Hearts

For more information, visit jljarvis.com.

Get monthly book news at news.jljarvis.com.

ABOUT THE AUTHOR

J.L. Jarvis is a left-handed former opera singer/teacher/lawyer who writes books. She now lives and writes on a mountaintop in upstate New York.

jljarvis.com

BOOK CLUB DISCUSSION QUESTIONS

A Cowboy Kind of Love

1. Bobby arrives at Cavanaugh Creek at a crossroads. She's built a good life in Tarrytown, but something feels slightly off. Have you ever had a moment where your life looked fine on paper but didn't quite fit? What finally made you pay attention to that feeling?
2. Bobby sees the world through her camera, and the story suggests that what she chooses to photograph reveals what she really feels long before she's ready to admit it. When did you first realize her camera was telling on her? Is there something in your own life that gives you away like that?
3. Wyatt is a man of very few words, but the ones he does say tend to land hard: "That's good," "I want it to be," "The ranch needs

one." Which of his lines hit you the hardest, and why do you think his silence makes the words he does speak carry so much weight?

4. Ruby is the emotional engine of the Cavanaugh family. She holds everyone together, feeds everyone, and sees everything before anyone else does. Did you find yourself wishing for more of her story? What do you think her relationship with Diego will look like going forward?
5. When Kay pitches "The Vanishing Ranch" story, she's not wrong. The piece could genuinely help family ranchers. Bobby has to choose between a story that could do real good and protecting the man she loves. Do you think she made the right call? Was there a version of this where she could have done both?
6. Judd barely speaks, but when he does — "You gonna let that one get away too?" — he changes the course of the whole story. Who is the Judd in your life, the person whose rare words carry the most weight?
7. The line shack scene during the storm is the emotional center of the book. Bobby and Wyatt are stripped down to who they really are: no cameras, no work, no excuses. What was it about that setting that finally let them be honest with each other? Have you ever had a moment where circumstances forced an honesty you'd been avoiding?

8. Bobby tells Wyatt, "I lost myself a little," and he says, "You got back up." The book treats getting back up not as a dramatic moment but as something quiet and ongoing. How does that compare to the way most stories handle heartbreak and recovery? Did Bobby's version feel more true to life?
9. Wyatt never chases Bobby to the airport. He sits on the bunkhouse bed with the photograph and lets her go. Were you frustrated with him in that moment, or did it feel true to who he is? What do you think changed between that night and the day he showed up in Tarrytown with the box?
10. The final image of the book is Bobby taking a photo of herself for the first time in three years. Why do you think that detail matters so much? What does it say about where she's landed, not just with Wyatt, but with herself?

www.ingramcontent.com/pod-product-compliance
Lightning Source LLC
LaVergne TN
LVHW091120080826
845145LV00008B/1988

9781942767930